ACROSS THE MIDDLE

LA WOLVES  BOOK TWO

CADENCE KEYS

Copyright © 2021 by Cadence Keys

All rights reserved.

No part of this book may be reproduced in any form or by any electronic or mechanical means, including information storage and retrieval systems, without written permission from the author, except for the use of brief quotations in a book review.

This book is a work of fiction. Names, characters, places, and incidents are a product of the author's imagination. Locales and public names are sometimes used for atmospheric purposes. Any resemblances to actual people, living or dead, businesses, companies, events, institutions, or locales are entirely coincidental. Any trademarks, service marks, product names, or named features are assumed to be the property of their respective owners and are used only for reference.

Editors: Happily Editing Anns

Cover Design: Kate Farlow, Y'all. That Graphic

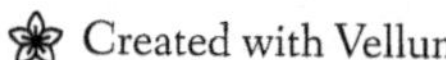 Created with Vellum

For every woman who's ever felt like she wasn't enough. You are enough. Always.

ONE

Will

I grab the neck of my beer bottle and bring it up to my lips, tipping it back and tasting the bitter hops that define this specific IPA. My eyes scan the room taking in the scene before me. There are waiters walking around with snacks and a bartender set up in the corner. Several players from our team are present to celebrate.

Jack and Paige have transformed their mansion into an elegant soiree to celebrate their engagement and New Year's Eve. I watch as Jack wraps his arm around Paige, a smile encompassing both their faces. I've never seen him look so happy. She's been one hell of a game changer for him.

I continue my perusal of the room until my gaze catches on a figure I recognize well—one I've been desperately trying to forget. Gina Rodrigo stands at the entrance of the room, and my heart pounds at the sight of her. I don't know what it is about this woman that sets my blood on fire, but every time we're in the same room, it's like no one exists but her. She's absolutely magnetic, and I'm getting really tired of fighting my body's response to her.

I'll never forget the first time I saw her. She walked out the doors of Paige's apartment building, smiled up at me, and twisted my entire existence on its axis. It was the first time in over a year I'd felt anything, and frankly, it was the first time in my life I'd had such a visceral reaction to a woman.

My gaze slides down her body. Her deep blue dress hugs every curve on her voluptuous frame. Everything about her calls to me, but I've been successful in fighting my attraction to her so far. I just need to continue to avoid her, which is easier said than done. Every time we've found ourselves thrown together this past year, I've been drawn to her. I always try to pull back, but something about her keeps me from pulling away completely, even when I know I should.

I take a deep breath, trying to find some composure. *She's just a woman.* Ah, if only that were true. The reality is Gina is so much more. She's vibrant and full of life. I won't be the one to drag her down.

My gaze slides back up her body, mesmerized by the café au lait color of her smooth, perfect skin. *God, what I would give to trace every inch of her body with my tongue.* But I'm not the guy that gets the woman of my dreams. Candace made sure of that.

The second her name slithers into my mind, guilt overwhelms me. How can I look at another woman after what happened with Candace? I've done so well being alone, with only the occasional meaningless fuck. I look down at the floor, wishing it would swallow me whole and all my guilt with me. I'm sick of the weight of it, but I can't let it go. Or it won't let me go—I'm not sure which anymore.

My skin prickles with awareness and I look up, my gaze crashing into Gina's, her light brown eyes holding mine hostage from across the room. My whole body aches to go to her, but I fight it with everything I have. I don't know how much longer I can battle this attraction to her. I've never felt this way before, but I know better than anyone that I don't deserve happiness, and I sure as hell don't deserve it with someone as effervescent as Gina.

She makes her way toward me, and I watch with both a desperation to escape and a yearning to make her mine in every way a woman can belong to a man. A year of repressed feelings is finally starting to overwhelm me. I need to get a fucking grip on this situation.

I take another pull from my beer, hoping it'll give me the strength to get through this night. I can't believe Jack talked me into coming to this New Year's Eve party. I haven't been to one since Candace died, and if it wasn't also his engagement party, I probably would've bailed and spent the night in my house watching the ball drop on my big-screen TV.

Gina comes to a stop two feet in front of me. I put my free hand in my pocket, so I won't be tempted to touch her. I use the other hand to bring my beer to my lips and take another swig.

"Will."

"Gina."

I watch her eyes scan my body and feel my blood rush south. It's been too long since I've been with a woman. I should be stronger than this.

"I didn't know you'd be here," she says as her eyes make their way back to mine, her cheeks slightly flushed.

My heart pumps harder in my chest at the hooded look in her eyes. Fuck, why couldn't she just hate me and make this easier?

I clear my throat and break eye contact, my eyes looking around the room. "I didn't expect you to be here, either. You didn't have any fun New Year's plans up in San Fran?"

"Paige was planning a big New Year's Eve thing before they got engaged, so I was already going to be here."

I look around the room. "That explains how they were able to pull this together so quickly."

Gina nods and looks at me closely, hesitating before she speaks. "It's good to see you. It's been awhile."

"A few months at least, right?" I act like I don't know, but I do. It's been four months. Jack and Paige invited everyone out for a big beach day before the weather changed. The image of Gina in her pink bikini has kept my right hand busy, not that she'll ever know.

"Yeah, September, when I came down for the beach weekend." She tucks a lock of her silky dark brown hair behind her ear, and my eyes catch on the diamond studs sitting elegantly on her lobes. She seems nervous, which throws me off. She's never been nervous around me before, at least not that I've noticed. She always comes across as strong and confident.

The only other time I've seen her less than confident was after a club event when she overheard me tell Max, Jack's best friend and assistant, I wasn't interested in her. It was a blatant lie, one she was never meant to hear.

The truth is I've been interested in Gina since the very first moment I saw her. But just because I'm interested doesn't mean I can ever have her. I can't. I don't deserve to be happy or fall in love, not after Candace.

I can't stand here much longer making pointless small talk. I'm already at the end of my rope just trying to keep myself from touching her.

"It's good to see you. If you'll excuse me, I need to go talk to Matt."

I ignore the brief moment of hurt on her face and make my way to my teammate Matt Fischer across the room. He's surrounded by a handful of women, and I'm hoping desperately one of them will be able to distract me from the only woman in this entire house who could ever truly capture my attention.

TWO

Gina

I stare at the space in front of me where Will was just standing. *What the hell was that?* I'm annoyed I can never get a read on him. One minute he's staring at me like he's starving and only I can sate his hunger, and the next he's looking at me like I have the power to absolutely destroy him and he's terrified I'll use it.

For over a year now, I've tried to figure him out, but the emotional whiplash is getting exhausting. I've tried to fight my attraction to Will Edmonson since it seemed pointless to give in to a man who lives six hours away from me. I've never wanted a long-distance relationship, and I sure as hell have no intention of wanting one now.

And yet, every time we're in the same room together, I'm drawn to him like a moth to a flame, just asking to get burned. Paige insinuated once that his last relationship ended badly, but she never clarified what that meant. I've been trying to get it out of her, but she won't spill, which means Jack swore her to secrecy, and after everything they went through when they first got together, I know she'd never betray his trust or break a promise to him.

I turn around just as Will reaches his teammate, who is surrounded by a bevy of gorgeous women. Jealousy burns in my gut when one skinny blonde tosses her head back with a laugh while placing her hand on Will's muscular arm.

I shake my head and look away, frustrated with myself for caring. Clearly, whatever attraction I thought was between us was one-sided. I grab a glass of champagne off a passing waiter's tray and make my way out to the patio. Walking over to the edge of the yard, I take in the view of Los Angeles.

I miss living in Southern California. I grew up in Long Beach with my three brothers and one sister. My mom has been begging me to find a journalist job in Los Angeles, but they aren't as easy to come by as she thinks. I work at an established paper—which is becoming less common due to the growing competition of the digital market—and I've worked hard to solidify my place with the Gazette. That being said, I miss working with Paige and hanging out with her all the time. It's definitely not been the same since she left.

"Great view, isn't it?"

The familiar voice pulls me from my thoughts, and I turn around with a smile on my face. "Max, always lovely to see you." I lean into him and give him a friendly peck on the cheek.

"How've you been?"

"Oh, you know me," he says, adding a flirtatious wink to his already charming smile. I can only imagine what that means. Max is an unrepentant flirt if ever there was one. But I don't know if that translates to actually being a player. I've never actually seen Max take a woman home, so who knows. Either way, it's never been like that between us. It's only ever been friendly flirting. Probably because my attention always goes to Will whenever we're all together. Max is perceptive and no doubt has picked up on my constant distraction.

"Party too much for ya?"

I look back out at the view. "No, it was fine. I just wanted some air."

"Uh-huh." I see him look back toward the house before looking back at me. "You wouldn't happen to be avoiding a certain wide receiver, would you?"

Like I said, perceptive.

"I'm not avoiding anyone. I said hello to Will earlier. He's the one who walked away to go hang out with another player." I think I do a decent job of hiding my hurt that Will abruptly ended our conversation.

"Idiot," Max mumbles, but I catch his word. I don't comment because I don't know what to say.

I've never wanted to be able to read people's minds before, but I'd pay all the money in the world to know what Will is thinking whenever we talk. Am I the only one who feels the chemistry between us? I can't be. I refuse to believe he doesn't feel it too. That his body doesn't feel like it's on fire with need whenever we're in the same room together.

A tingle at the base of my neck causes a small shiver to race down my spine, and the feeling someone's watching me causes me to turn around. My eyes find Will's almost instantly. Despite the fact he's still in the house against the wall farthest from me, our gazes are locked on each other. Heat spreads through me as I let my gaze slide down his form. Will is impossibly sexy, but not arrogant about it like most professional athletes are. My eyes peruse his fit, six-foot, three-inch frame. The man clearly never skips a gym day. He has inky-black hair my fingers ache to grip. His physique is every woman's fantasy, but it isn't what grabs my attention; it's his piercing green eyes that always call to me.

When our eyes lock on each other, I feel drawn to him. I pat Max on the arm and offer a quick goodbye before I make my way through the crowd to Will. He works his way toward me like we're two magnets drawn together, and we end up meeting right outside the patio doors. Shouts and cheers from inside the house catch my attention as people start counting down to midnight.

How is it midnight already? I let my gaze glide back to Will as his fingers slide across my cheek. My breath catches in my chest at the gentle gesture. I search for some explanation for this sudden change in behavior, but all I see in his jade-green eyes is need. A need that matches my own.

He *does* feel this connection between us. The relief at not being alone in this is immense. I let my eyes flutter closed, anticipating a midnight kiss, waiting to hear everyone finish the New Year's Eve countdown. I'm desperate to feel Will's lips on mine. Maybe he'll finally be able to sate this desire that has grown in me since we first met.

Three, two, one!

The cheers are muffled as people kiss and then wish each other a happy New Year. When I still don't feel Will's lips, I open my eyes only to see the most pained and haunted look on his face. Any desire that had been there is long gone. Hell, if I hadn't seen it up close, I would've thought I imagined any affection for me at all.

My heart plummets to my stomach. His hand pulls away from my face, leaving me feeling colder than a Chicago winter.

He shakes his head, despair filling his eyes. "I'm sorry. I can't."

With those whispered words, he turns and flees. I stand there, bereft of the joy and anticipation I had felt only moments before. What changed in three seconds?

I take a deep, cleansing breath, and work to refortify my walls that Will always manages to break down with just a look. I can't let that happen again. In all the times we've done this dance in the last year, he's never left me feeling so dejected.

I compose myself and feel my shields rise. I need to stop whatever this is with him. I've been played with enough by the previous men I've dated. I don't need it from him too.

After tonight, I'm more certain than ever. Will Edmonson and I will never work.

Will

The laughter around me faded as she smiled at me, her eyes sparking with a mischief that made me feel like I was in on a secret with her. I couldn't help but match her smile with one of my own. Her hand reached out and grazed my arm seductively, making her intentions clear. Celebrating a victory with my buddies usually meant going out for drinks and heading home alone, but for the first time in a long time, I wanted what she was offering. I wanted to get lost in between her legs and hear what sounds I could make come out of that lush mouth of hers.

With a nod toward the door, I said, "So, Candace, you wanna get out of here?"

With a smile full of promise of the good things to come, she replied, "I thought you'd never ask."

The barking around me tells me to keep my options open, but I can't move away from the dog in front of me.

"That's Rex. He's a pit bull, which as you can see, we have a lot of. There's a really negative stereotype that sticks with them, but I've found them to be some of the most loving dogs I've ever worked with."

I nod to acknowledge I heard Anita, the shelter worker, but I still can't break away from Rex. His eyes connect with mine, and instantly it's like I've found a kindred spirit. He looks as lost and broken as I feel.

Anita speaks again. "Rex has been here for months. He was an owner surrender. A man brought him in after he lost his job. Said they couldn't afford to have a pet anymore, and he had to sneak Rex out while his kids were asleep so they wouldn't yell at him about it. Damn near broke my heart watching Rex whine when the man left. He's been despondent the whole time he's been here, but pits are so hard to rehome."

I stare at Rex and absorb the information she's just laid on me. Rex and I are two of a kind. We've both been hurt by people we thought we could trust. People we thought loved us.

I don't need to look at any more dogs. In fact, I don't think I *can* look at any more without wanting to rescue all of them.

"I'll take him."

I smile to myself as Rex and I walk down the aisle of the pet store. He has a pep in his step that was missing when I first saw him at the shelter. It warms my heart and eases some of the residual ache and guilt that has held my body hostage since leaving Gina abruptly a few days ago.

I wanted to kiss her so desperately I could feel it in my bones, but as soon as she closed her eyes, all I saw was Candace glaring at me. That visual in my mind put my entire body on lockdown, and it was exactly the wakeup call I needed to pull back from Gina. The hurt and confusion in her eyes mirrored what I was feeling inside. But as much as I want her, I can't go there with her. Not now, not ever.

Rex nuzzles his nose against a thick rope lying in one of the bottom bins. "You want this toy, Rex?"

"I'd get a Kong or two, if I were you. The black ones." I turn to the female voice a couple of feet down the aisle from me.

"Why is that?"

She smiles at Rex and then I watch her eyes roam up my body before meeting mine. "I have two pitties, and trust me, that rope won't last very long. Hell, the so called 'indestructible' black Kong probably won't last either, but it holds up much better than any other toy I've found."

I look at the rope now securely in Rex's mouth and then up to the Kong toys she's pointed out. "Maybe I'll get him all three."

"Can I pet him?"

I nod, and she steps forward, bends down, and holds her hand out to him. "How old is he?"

"The lady at the shelter said he was about three years old."

The woman glances up at me seductively from her lowered position. "You rescued him?" There's heat in her tone, and from this position it's easy to imagine what she'd look like on her knees looking up at me for a very different reason. But I don't feel a single thing. My body doesn't light up for her like it does when I see a certain voluptuous brunette.

And now I'm thinking about Gina again and how fucking gorgeous she looked at that damn New Year's Eve party. Fuck me, why can't I get her out of my mind?

"Did you hear me?"

I'm pulled from my thoughts by the woman's hand on my arm. "Sorry, I'm a bit distracted today."

She smiles flirtatiously. "Oh, well, I was just suggesting we get our pitties together for a play date. Dogs are social creatures, and it would give us a chance to get to know each other better."

She slides her fingers up and down my arm. She's attempting to appear sexy, but she's being way too forward for my taste. Plus, I have no idea if this woman knows who I am. For all I know, she's a jersey chaser who's taking advantage of an opportunity. I move away from her, grabbing two big black Kongs from the display and the rope Rex has in his mouth, and then walk backwards out of the aisle.

"I think Rex and I need to get comfortable with each other before we introduce anyone else to the mix. Thanks for the advice about the toys. Have a good day."

With that, I turn around and get the rest of the items I need to make sure Rex is comfortable in his new home.

I sit down on the couch after picking up the shreds from the rope Rex has already destroyed.

"I still can't believe you got a dog."

I look up at Matt as he walks into my living room from the kitchen with a beer in each hand.

"I've always wanted one, and it seemed like a good time."

I don't tell him the main reason was because I couldn't stand being in my house alone with my thoughts anymore, and a dog seemed like the safest choice of companion.

He hands me my beer and plops down on the other side of the couch. "So, what game tape are we watching today?"

"I was thinking the game against the Saints since we play them next week."

With the remote in my right hand and a beer in the left, I pull up the game footage on my big-screen TV, while Rex lies on his new dog bed, a Kong in his mouth. I'm comforted by how happy and content he appears. The dog I first met at the shelter is long gone, and I can't help but envy how easy it was for him to let me in. We've bonded already, to the point where he rarely lets me out of his sight. I'll need to ask my sister Becka if she can watch him when I go to away games, but if she can't, I know our sister Lainey will.

Rex yawns and then stares at me. He gets out of his bed and makes his way over to me, placing his head in my lap and giving me the most pathetically needy eyes I've ever seen.

"You're an ASPCA commercial come to life, aren't you, buddy?"

He places his paw on my leg next to his head.

"You want on the couch?"

He perks right up, and I know that's exactly what he wants. "Alright, Rex, come on." I pat the couch cushion in between Matt and me. He jumps up without hesitation before curling up at my side, his head on my lap. I set down the remote and rub behind his ears, still wrapping my head around how quickly he's changed.

I want so badly to be able to be this relaxed with someone. How lame is it that I'm jealous of a dog? He was able to let go of his past and accept me without any hesitation.

"Dude, you really need to get a woman. As much as I love dogs, I'd much rather have a woman's head in my lap."

"You mean you'd rather have her mouth on your dick."

He smiles, unashamed of his playboy ways. "Isn't that what I just said?"

I shake my head and continue to scratch Rex's ears. I try to focus on the game tape we're supposed to be watching but get lost in my own thoughts.

I went to that shelter seeking companionship, hoping it would reduce the ache in my heart at my need for Gina.

Instead, all it's done is make me think maybe I'm getting in my own way. Maybe I should just let Gina rescue me.

Maybe Matt is right—minus the whole sexual innuendo, not that I'd say no to Gina's mouth on me.

I lay my head back against the couch. Yeah, Gina would definitely rescue me, but at what cost? She doesn't deserve someone as broken as me. She deserves a guy who can give her the whole world, and no matter how desperately I wish I was that guy, I'm not. I'm just a broken man with a dead fiancée, and my guilt would eventually crush us both. I refuse to hurt Gina that way.

FOUR

Gina

It's been two weeks since I returned from LA determined to forget about Will Edmonson. As soon as I got back, I caved and told Selene, a coworker friend of mine, I would go on a blind date with her boyfriend's friend, Peter. She'd been hassling me for months to give him a shot. Apparently, she thought we would be perfect for each other. I have my doubts.

I'm not new to blind dates. I've been on several in the past, and not a single one has turned out well. I have more success with online dating, but I find it exhausting and superficial. Successful dating ultimately comes down to chemistry, and good chemistry with a man is hard to find.

I walk up to the hostess stand. "Hi, I'm meeting a Peter Savine. I'm not sure if he's arrived yet."

She checks her book. "Yep, he showed up just a minute ago and was seated at your table. Right this way."

I take a deep breath, trying to be open-minded about this date and not think about the one man who's never far from my thoughts no matter how hard I try. This is a new start full of possibilities. A chance to meet someone who doesn't leave me feeling confused about what he wants. That thought settles in my mind as the hostess leads me through the restaurant. Ahead of us, I see a man clearly flirting with the waitress, his hand caressing hers.

"Well, those are bedroom eyes if ever I saw some. Does that happen often?" I ask the hostess. She turns to me with an awkward grimace on her face I don't understand until we stop at that very table and she gestures to the man. "Your table, ma'am."

Oh God, she threw a "ma'am" in there. Now, not only do I feel like I'm on a date with a lecherous playboy, but I also feel old. The feeling of possibility that carried me over here is quickly eviscerated. The waitress scurries away, and I watch Peter's eyes follow her ass before turning back to me and throwing a charismatic grin my way.

Yeah, no.

I should go. This is clearly not going to be a love connection. But instead of doing the smart thing, I find myself taking a seat across from him.

He's polite and respectful and asks how long I've known Selene. I desperately want to let my guard down and allow myself to enjoy this date, but every time the waitress comes over, he blatantly flirts with her. When he caresses her hand again right in front of me, I finally lose my cool.

"What the hell is wrong with you?"

"Excuse me?" He seems legitimately confused by my angry question.

"You've been flirting with the waitress in front of me all night. Is that a normal occurrence for you when you're out on dates with other women? Because I'm not interested in dating a man who can't be faithful."

He looks at me curiously for a long moment before leaning back in his chair. "Selene didn't tell you."

His tone makes me nervous. "Tell me what?"

He leans forward again. "I'm polyamorous."

I stare at him, hoping he'll elaborate. Instead, he simply stares back at me like that one word explains everything. It doesn't.

"I don't know what that means."

He puts on a condescending smirk like you would give to a small child when you think they're precious but pitifully naïve. Immediately, I hate it and how he makes me feel stupid with one look. If I wanted to be looked down on by some condescending dickhead, I'd still be with my ex. Any of my exes for that matter.

"Polyamory means I like to have intimate relationships with multiple people. I thought you knew, or else I would've talked to you about it before flirting so openly with the waitress. Polyamory only truly works if everyone involved is honest and open about our intentions and interests in others."

I stare at him dumbfounded. How have I never heard of this before? I feel like this date has turned into a new low for me.

I try to wrap my head around this. "Selene knows you're..." I can't even say the word. It feels ridiculous.

"Polyamorous," he supplies.

"Right," I say uncomfortably.

"Yes, Selene knows. Or at least I thought she did, but now I'm not so sure based on your reaction. That seems like something she would've told you before you agreed to this."

"Yes, it does," I respond stiffly. I need to get out of this situation. I should've never even sat down at this table.

I grab my purse and stand from my chair. "It was lovely meeting you, Peter, but I don't think this is going to work. I'm a one-man kind of woman and I expect the same from him. Best of luck to you."

With that, I turn and walk away, not even waiting for a response from him. What's the point?

As soon as I get in my house, I call Paige. I had plenty of time on the drive home to process, but I still need my best friend.

She picks up on the third ring. "Hey! Wait, didn't you have a date tonight? It's only eight."

"Have you heard of polyamory?"

"Random, but yeah, I've heard of it. It's a more modern relationship thing. I think it was started by millennials but don't quote me on that. Why?"

"He's polyamorous."

"No way!"

"Yes way," I sigh heavily. My dating life has been a disaster for years, but tonight really took it to a whole other level. Not only do I have to compete with gorgeous, successful women, but now I'm competing with women who don't believe in exclusivity and will allow their man to sleep with whomever he wants. As if finding a man to commit wasn't hard enough already.

"How did you find out he was poly?"

I rub my forehead, hoping to stop the headache that is coming on quickly. "Well, he was blatantly flirting with our waitress. When I called him on it, he told me. He apparently thought I already knew."

"How could you have possibly known?" I love that Paige sounds outraged on my behalf. "Also, I'm pretty sure that's not how poly relationships are supposed to work. There's supposed to be a lot of communication with everyone involved. At least that's what I've heard."

"He thought Selene would've told me."

"Selene knew?! And she set you up with him still?"

"I don't think she knows. There's no way she could've

thought we'd be a love connection. I'm a traditionalist. I'll ask her at work tomorrow."

"I can hear the defeat in your tone. Keep your chin up, Gina. The right guy for you is out there."

I stare out my windows, wishing I had a better view, but San Francisco is ridiculously expensive, so I live outside the city in nearby San Jose. Still expensive, but better. My small house I share with roommates overlooks a city park, but it doesn't compare to having a view of the Golden Gate Bridge. Unfortunately, houses with that kind of view are *way* out of my price range.

"Maybe he was hit by a car," I say blandly.

"What?" Paige laughs awkwardly at my out-of-the-blue thought.

"Maybe my so-called Mr. Right was hit by a car, or a bus, or a train, and now I'm just wasting my time because no one out there is the right one."

"Gina, that's an incredibly depressing thought. Besides...I happen to think your Mr. Right is alive and well but living in a different city than you."

I groan, "Stop, Paige."

"Whaaat?" She feigns innocence but I'm on to her.

"I know who you're talking about, and you're wrong."

"How do you know? You and Will haven't even gone on a date yet. Everyone can feel the chemistry between you two. I really think once you're living in LA, you two will finally put us all out of our misery and get together."

She's so optimistic, but she didn't see his eyes on New Year's. I can't get the haunted expression on his face out of my mind.

"Speaking of moving, did you give any more thought to Victoria's offer to work at Newsworthy? You could live closer to your family, and we could work together again." She can't hide the excitement in her voice.

"I'm thinking about it."

Victoria Hunt, Paige's boss at Newsworthy, offered me a job as a full-time reporter. They're a growing digital media news source, and Paige has never seemed happier at a job. There's a lot about the job that appeals to me, but I'm still not sure. I don't really know why I'm hesitating. The opportunity is perfect for me. Maybe Paige is right, not about Will, but about the benefits of taking this position.

"It would be nice to be in the same city again. I miss you, Gina."

I smile. "I miss you too." And ain't that the truth? Paige is my best friend. I drive down to LA fairly regularly just to visit her. It would definitely be a major perk to live in the same city and be able to see her whenever I want. Plus, my mom is still hassling me about moving closer to the rest of my family.

"I'll think about calling Victoria." Paige squeals in the background, causing me to laugh. "Okay, calm down. Nothing is a done deal yet. It'll probably take a few weeks to get everything squared away and then I'll have to find an apartment and get all my stuff moved."

"Jack and I will help," she volunteers.

"Good, 'cause I'll definitely need all the help I can get."

I look around my house, feeling hope and optimism settle deep in my bones. This is the right decision. This change will be good—I can feel it.

FIVE

Will

Our plane lands at San Jose International Airport, and we make our way to the hotel. The Wolves are playing the Niners tomorrow in the divisional round of playoff games, so we get the night to explore the area around Levi's Stadium. A group of rookies head to San Francisco, while the rest of us decide to hang around San Jose. I learned a long time ago that if I didn't want to draw attention to myself, it was best if I wandered around on my own. I leave the rest of the guys to figure out what their plans are and make my way to Santana Row. There's an amazing candy shop there I stumbled on my first time here, and I always make sure to stop in whenever I'm up here.

I'm a sucker when it comes to candy. It's been that way since I was a little boy and would hoard my Halloween and Easter candy. I never overindulged, but I definitely enjoyed every last bite. Okay, that's a lie. I might've overindulged a few times, but come on, I was a kid. What kid doesn't overdo it on their Halloween candy?

I make my way down the sidewalk with my baseball cap pulled low and my head down, hoping I can be a little incognito.

I'm just about to turn toward the door of Sugarfina when I bump into a woman, knocking her coffee right out of her hand.

"Oh shit. I'm so sorry," I say as I reach down to pick up her cup.

"Will?"

My heart stops at the sound of her voice. I look up into the face of the woman I've been fantasizing about for a year. The woman whose confused eyes have been haunting my waking thoughts since New Year's Eve.

"Gina."

The word escapes my mouth on a disbelieving breath. Of all the places I would see her, I run into her here.

"I thought you lived in San Francisco?" I ask as I stand, tossing her wasted coffee cup into a nearby trash can.

She shakes her head. "No, it's too expensive to live in the city on a reporter's salary. I commute to the Gazette and live here in San Jose. It's still criminal what they charge for rent, but cheaper than living closer to work. As it is, I live with room-mates just to afford it." She pauses, then continues, "Sorry, I'm rambling. I didn't expect to see you here."

She bites her lip, and the action damn near brings me to my knees. What I wouldn't give to be the one to bite that lip. I try to get the image out of my head, but her honey-brown eyes surrounded by thick black lashes hold me captive, and now all I can think about are her eyes staring at me while her mouth does something very different. Gina looks at me expectantly, and I realize she's waiting for an explanation.

"We're playing the 49ers tomorrow. We just got into town."

She nods her head like that makes perfect sense. She starts looking around and opens her mouth like she's about to say something, but I cut her off.

"I'm sorry about your coffee. Let me make it up to you. Do you like candy?"

She hesitates. "I should really probably head home."

"Do you have other plans?" I suspect she doesn't, but I don't want to be pushy if she does.

She bites her lip again, looking at me like she's trying to figure me out. *Get in line, honey.* I don't know why I'm torturing myself. I know being around Gina is a terrible idea, but now that she's standing in front of me, I feel a desperate need to keep her here.

"No, I don't have other plans."

The tension in my shoulders fades. "Do you like candy?"

She gives me a small smile that makes me feel fifty feet tall. "If you're talking about Sugarfina candy, then count me in. I love that place."

I smile back at her and, without thinking, offer her my hand. She looks at it for a moment, a look on her face I can't quite place, before she sticks her hands in the pockets of her peacoat and turns toward the door of Sugarfina. Her rejection stings, but I bury it quickly and open the door for her to walk through.

I'm always taken aback by the elegance of this place. It has to be the fanciest candy shop I've ever seen. The bright white interior walls and lights allow for the vibrant colors of the various candies and the bold turquoise of the bento boxes to stand out. Along the walls, candies are organized by their color palette, and it's a rainbow display unlike any other.

"So, what's your favorite candy?"

She throws me a soft smile. "Hmm...probably the chocolate covered cookie dough. But I've been dying to try the salted caramel gelato candies. How can you beat the flavors of ice cream in a candy?"

"You can't. I've been wanting to try those too, especially the mint chip flavor. It's my favorite." I grin down at her. God, she's beautiful. For a moment, I wish this was a date.

The thought takes me by surprise, but I can't stop the

warmth that spreads through my body at the idea of taking Gina out on a real date. I stop at a row of candies while Gina continues perusing the selection, but instead of looking at the sweet treats in front of me, my attention is captivated by her. Longing like I've never known overwhelms me.

It was never like this with Candace.

I'm ashamed of the thought, but it's true. What I felt for Candace doesn't even hold a candle to how I feel about Gina.

SIX

Gina

Of all the people for me to run into tonight. I shake my head as I continue to peruse the candy selection. I try to subtly glance behind me, but my efforts are wasted when I look up and my gaze instantly connects with Will. A subtle blush floods his cheeks, but he doesn't look away. My chest tightens as blood pumps furiously to my rapidly beating heart. Tingles spread down my body as longing pulses deep in my core.

God, the look on that man's face is pure sex. A quick flash of guilt fills his eyes and then he finally breaks our connection.

And there it is.

The reason I can't keep doing this same old dance with him.

He always pulls away.

I want a man who will fight for me. How hard is that to find? The answer: apparently impossible. I blame fairy tales. They filled our little girl minds with the belief the prince will go door to door just to find the one woman who fits the glass slipper. But that's not real life. Men don't chase women. They just sit back and take the ones that are easy. Heaven forbid they have to actually put any effort into their relationships.

It's some seriously passive bullshit that really irritates the crap out of me. I feel my temper rising and work to tamp it down. I've had to learn how to control my short fuse since it's not appreciated in the journalism world. My tenacity is necessary, but patience is something else reporters need to have. They need to know when to dig and ask questions, but also when to keep their mouth shut so someone else will try to fill the silence. Several of my biggest stories have come from me being able to outlast a prolonged silence.

But that isn't the case here with Will. I don't even know what we're doing. I look over at him and watch him fill a bento box with some candies. I wish I could outlast him, but the reality is Will scares the shit out of me. And that fear pulls me between wanting to run fast and far away from him, or attempting to fill the silence with my own rambling in the hopes he'll finally take this—whatever *this* is—in a more serious direction.

I've never responded to a man the way I do with Will. And that's terrifying because it means he has the ability to break me worse than any other man ever has. And I have no doubt that's exactly what he'd do, if his constant hot and cold demeanor is any indication.

Despite my resolution that I can't keep playing this back and forth with him, the moment I feel Will's heat warm my back, my whole body lights up.

"I bought us a couple of things," he whispers, his warm breath cascading down my neck.

A shiver slides across my body. His quick inhale tells me he noticed. I'm trying to remind myself why this is a bad idea, but then Will gently grazes my fingers with his own. He takes a step forward, his front pressing lightly against my back. My eyes fall closed as I absorb the most delicious sensation of having his big, strong body behind me. His head leans down and his nose rests against my hair.

"You smell fucking amazing." The hoarseness of his tone sets my body on fire, and suddenly the only thought in my brain is that I have to get this man naked.

I desperately want to turn around and take his mouth with mine, but then I'm reminded of what happened on New Year's Eve. I think I'll die a little inside if I have to see that look in his eyes again, so instead, I fight my body's desire and stay completely still. I soak in his warmth and the feeling of completeness that spreads through me.

There's always been an invisible string tying Will and me together, but touching him, even just like this, takes it up a notch.

His lips press lightly right behind my ear, and I can't prevent the low moan that releases from my throat. He matches it with his own groan in response and then whispers in my ear.

"I don't want to fight this anymore." He kisses my neck. "I want you, Gina."

My heart soars at his words and relief fills my body. Oh God, the relief. I was seriously starting to think I was alone in this, but he really does feel it too. This undeniable connection is definitely mutual if his erection is any indication. I can feel his hardness pressing firmly against my back.

"Candace! Get back here." A mother scolds her child near us, and I'm reminded we're in the middle of a candy shop. Will must've realized the same thing, because he abruptly pulls away from me.

I turn around, a flirty smile on my face, prepared to suggest we grab a bite to eat and then head back to his hotel room, because I definitely don't want our first time together to be within earshot of my nosy roommates. But when I look up at him, my smile falters.

"Will? What's wrong?" He's looking at the mother and daughter near us, the same ones who interrupted our moment, but he looks like he's seen a ghost. His face is white, his eyes wide, and he seems to be completely frozen in place.

"Will?" I place my hand soothingly on his arm, but the second I make contact, he rips his arm away and looks at me with a look that is all too familiar. That look filled with pain like he's haunted by something dark.

I don't break eye contact with him. "What just happened? Just a minute ago, you were about to—"

"That was a mistake."

He might as well have slapped me. Hurt and embarrassment fill me. My eyes sting with oncoming tears, but I refuse to let them fall. I will not let this man see me break.

I clench my jaw and nod my head slowly, buying myself a little time to make sure when I speak, my voice won't crack from the emotion I'm fighting.

"You know what? You're absolutely right. It was a mistake. One I will *never* make again."

Without another word, I turn and walk out of Sugarfina, my head held high, while my heart falls lower with every step.

Will doesn't follow.

As much as I want to hate him, the only thing I feel is a desperate need to understand what happened and what continues to keep him from actually giving us a shot. There's a connection between us that for some reason is damn near impossible to sever. Even now, when I should be more determined than ever to never see or speak to him again, I still feel that connection. All I know is my heart wants him with a blinding loyalty that is frustrating and frankly undeserved.

Unfortunately, the heart wants what the heart wants. With the painful realization my heart has chosen a completely unattainable man to fall for, I get to my car and drive home, hoping someday I'll finally be able to let him go.

SEVEN

Will

I stared at the text on my phone, debating how to reply.

"If you stare at your phone any harder, you're going to burn a hole in it."

I looked up to see Jack and Matt staring at me with matching expressions of curiosity.

"I bet you twenty bucks it's a chick," Matt said with a smug smile on his face.

Jack looked at me questioningly, probably wanting me to dispute the suggestion made by our playboy teammate, but for the first time since I'd been drafted, I couldn't. Matt was right.

I looked back down at the text from Candace, my jaw shifting back and forth as I thought about what to say. I'd never had a girlfriend before, and had never even really been drawn to anyone like I was with her. I didn't want to say the wrong thing.

Candace was vibrant and fun, always the life of the party, and always with a smile on her face. For the first time, it wasn't just about sex with a woman. It was about her.

I looked up at my friends, "You guys remember the woman from the bar after we won that game against the Broncos?"

"The hot blonde with the great rack?"

"Yeah, Matt, that would be the one."

Both guys nodded.

"What about her?" Jack asked.

"Wait, are you still seeing her?" Matt asked.

"Yeah, we've been catching time together whenever I'm in town." I paused, trying to find a way to frame this without sounding like a total pussy. "I really like her and I'm thinking of pursuing a relationship with her."

"Why?" Matt asked, his face morphed in complete and utter confusion.

Jack immediately slapped him on the chest. "Not everyone is content with a new fuck every night like you. Some of us prefer regular sex."

Matt shrugged and then tossed us a salacious smirk. "A new chick every night is still regular pussy, if you want to get technical about it."

Jack rolled his eyes at him before he turned to me. "Are you sure she's not a jersey chaser?"

"Yeah, I'm fairly positive. She's different, Jack. It's hard to explain, but there's just something about her. And I know for a fact she's not after me for my money because her parents are loaded, so there's nothing to worry about there."

He slapped me on the back. "Then I say go for it. When you find the woman you want, you shouldn't let her go." He dropped his eyes to the floor, like his words meant more to him than he planned for them to.

"You really think so?"

He nodded and then went back to getting changed for our game. I looked back down at my phone and without questioning it further, I shot Candace a text asking her if she was free tomorrow.

I throw the stick for Rex and watch him pump his legs at a frantic pace to get it.

"That is one spoiled dog."

I turn to the familiar voice and smile at my sister, Becka. "Hey, Becks, what are you doing here?"

"Oh, you know. Just thought I'd take a stroll."

"Really?" I ask doubtfully.

"No, not really. I was driving to your house and noticed you when I passed by the park."

I laugh. "Yeah, that makes more sense."

Of my three sisters, Becka and I have always been the closest, which also means she's nosier than the others and always trying to get in my business. She's also the only one who lives in LA. Lainey lives in Laguna Beach, and the rest of my family still live back in Texas.

We stand together quietly while I continue to throw the stick every time Rex brings it back. She finally breaks the silence.

"I'm worried about you, Will."

I turn to her. "Nothin' to worry about, Becks."

She looks at me, her brows pinched with concern. "Lie to yourself all you want, but don't lie to me."

I look at her, then look back out at the field, my jaw clenched tight with the anger that's been simmering just beneath the surface for days. I know where she's going with this, and I'm not ready to go there, especially not after what happened last week in San Jose with Gina.

God, the look on her face when I said it was a mistake gutted me. Even thinking about it right now makes me feel like the lowest scum of the earth. The truth is, it wasn't a mistake at all. It was a fucking dream, and once again Candace ruined it.

The fucking bitch is dead, and she's still making my life hell.

That thought makes my stomach curl. God, I'm a terrible

human being. I can't believe I just thought that, when it's *my* fault she's dead. My familiar companion, guilt, washes over me.

"The look on your face is why I'm so worried about you."

I turn to see Becks staring at me, her arms crossed like she's prepared for me to put up a fight about it. But I know she's right to be worried.

I think about Gina again and how badly I've fucked everything up with her. There's something between us that is terrifying to me, but at the same time I'm starting to feel like I need her in order to breathe. Like she was always meant to be mine.

I shove the thought aside, especially since odds are she'll never be mine after what I said to her.

"I'm not ready, okay? I get why you're worried, but I can't go there."

"It's been two years, Will. Why are you holding on so tightly to someone who never deserved you in the first place?"

Becka made her feelings about Candace very clear when Candace and I first got together. When we got engaged, I thought Becka was going to stop speaking to me, she was so furious. From the beginning, she saw what I couldn't until it was too late.

I shrug my shoulders at her question. I'm not ready to admit my role in what happened the night Candace died. For two years, I've held on to my guilt and let it fester. I've never told a single soul what really happened the last time I saw Candace.

"That's not an answer. If you won't tell me, then maybe you should see a professional. Either way, you have to talk about this. I can tell it's eating you alive. You don't deserve that, Will."

Oh, but I do.

"You deserve to fall in love with a woman who can truly love you. A woman who makes your heart soar and makes you feel like you can't function without her."

I instantly picture Gina, and my heart aches. I attempt to

ignore it. "I think you've been reading too many romance novels again. That's not real life."

I can't take the look of pity on her face while she absorbs my words, so I turn back to Rex and let him distract me.

"You know what's really sad? It is real life, Will. Yes, people every day settle for so much less than they deserve. They settle for love that feels safe, but there's a difference between safety because you're not risking your heart and safety because you know your heart is being held with care by the one you love. Too many people settle for the former, when they should hold out for the latter."

"When did you get so wise about love?"

"When I experienced the difference."

That gets my attention. "What? I didn't know you were seeing anyone."

"I'm not," she says sadly, and all my big brother instincts go on high alert.

"Did someone break your heart? Whose ass do I need to kick?"

She smiles sadly at me. "I'm a big girl, Will. I don't need my brother to fight my battles. I'm handling it. But it's made me think about you and your situation. It kills me seeing you torture yourself over Candace. She doesn't deserve that loyalty, especially when she wasn't even loyal to you."

"Becks, stop, please. I'm just not ready yet."

"I'm worried if you wait until you're ready, you might miss out on the real thing."

I'm worried too. I'm worried I might've already lost the real thing, and I'm not talking about Candace.

EIGHT

Gina

Late August

I pull up to my parents' Long Beach house, exhausted from a long day of apartment hunting. I try to stop by their house whenever I'm down in LA to visit Paige, but it's been almost a month since I was here last.

I open the door with the key my parents insisted I keep for my visits and am immediately greeted by a room full of my mother's closest friends.

"Gina! Did your mother know you were coming? What am I asking? Of course she didn't know, or else she would've had a party! Or tried to set you up with someone from the neighborhood." She whispers the last part conspiratorially, and I can't help but laugh at my mother's best friend, Maria.

"You know my mother too well, Titi." She smiles at the term of endearment commonly used for all Puerto Rican "aunts"— the women you aren't related to by blood but who are practically family anyway.

"Gina?" My mother walks out of the kitchen, drying her

hands with a towel. "Honey, it's so good to see you. What brings you down here?"

"Well, I have some good news." I smile and shake my head when I realize all activity in the room has stopped at my announcement. It's not often I get this kind of undivided attention. I'm not the first girl of the family, but I'm not the baby either. That leaves me as an awkward middlish child, and having four siblings and a house full of family and friends meant I spent most of my life trying to be seen or heard, often ineffectually.

"Well?" my mom prods.

"I got a job working with Paige at Newsworthy in LA. I've been apartment hunting all day and will be moving down here permanently in about two weeks."

"Wepa!" Maria calls out in celebration and the room erupts with cheers while I get passed around receiving a hug from everyone in the room.

When I make my way back to my mother, she's beaming and cups my cheek. "My sweet little Cochita. It'll be so good to have you close again." I hug my mom and smile to myself that she still calls me her little cupcake. It started with one of my uncles calling me Bizcochito once because I was so obsessed with cupcakes as a child, but quickly got condensed, made feminine and became a permanent nickname for me.

I spend the rest of the day celebrating with my mom and her friends, laughing at their banter with each other. It feels good to be surrounded by family, and excitement courses through me knowing I'll be able to see them more frequently once I've moved down here.

I stay the night in my old room, surrounded by memories of childhood. Growing up in a large family isn't always easy. It can sometimes be exhausting trying to find ways to stand out from your siblings and cousins, but there's a never-ending abundance of love and tradition in this house that soothes me in a way I haven't felt in quite a while.

I glance at the picture frame on my nightstand of my abuela and me from a summer trip to Puerto Rico when I was twelve. I smile softly as I trace my finger along the frame, remembering how hard the visit was for me. I had felt so lost in my family. My brothers were all athletic and shining stars in their chosen sports, my sister was smart and excelled in school, while I felt like the awkward ugly duckling that didn't belong. I was terribly uncoordinated, and I barely managed Cs.

That summer, my siblings all had a lot going on, and my parents were planning to drag me around to all their different events, where I was sure I would be ignored. I begged my parents to let me spend the summer in Puerto Rico with my abuela instead, and after a lot of pleading, they finally relented. It was one of the best summers I've ever had.

Abuela has always made me feel special, even when I had a hard time finding my place in my family. She got me. She understood me. She knew my struggles. That summer, she became one of my best friends and confidantes.

An ache tugs at my heart. I wish she would move to Long Beach so I could see her more, but she refuses to leave Puerto Rico. She says it's her home and the only home she plans to have. She was born there, and she'll die there. The thought alone guts me. I'm not ready to lose her. I try to talk to her at least once a week, but it never feels like enough.

I gently place the frame back on my nightstand and fall asleep dreaming of Puerto Rico. The next morning, my mom insists on making me breakfast before I head back to San Francisco.

"So, are you excited about this change?"

"Yeah, I think it'll be good. Things have been getting really expensive in San Jose, and working at the paper hasn't been the same since Paige left."

My mother nods. "You have been two peas in a pod since college. I'm glad you've stayed such good friends. She's a sweet girl. How are things going with that man of hers?"

I smile. "They're still doing great. As in love as ever last time I talked to her. They're the real deal."

"And how about you, Cochita? Are there any men in your life?"

I hate that Will's face flits through my mind. But like the man himself, my body goes cold and the thought disappears quickly. "No, no men lately, mami."

"Are they all gay in San Francisco?" she asks seriously, and I almost spit my orange juice out at her ridiculous question.

"Mom!"

"What?" She's genuinely confused.

I can't stop the laugh that pops out. "No, the men in San Francisco are not all gay. I just don't seem to have any luck finding men who are willing to commit to me."

My mother scoffs, surely thinking about Andrew and Collin, both exes who had a penchant for cheating on me and then blaming me for it. I don't know how guys get away with that excuse. It is not the woman's fault if he can't keep his dick in his pants and chooses to be unfaithful.

"Well, maybe you'll have better luck finding a good man down here," she says hopefully. My mom would love for me to settle down and give her more grandchildren. I thought I was off the hook when my older siblings all started having children, but no such luck. She won't be content until she sees all her babies married off with babies of their own. The idea appeals to me for sure, but I just can't seem to find my very own Prince Charming.

Her comment makes me think of Will again. "Maybe if we were Irish I'd have better luck."

"The Irish don't have the market cornered on luck, Gina. Sometimes you have to make your own luck. The right man for you is out there, and when you're both ready, life will find a way to put you two together. But in the meantime, you can do your part by putting yourself out there so life can put him in your path."

Thinking back on the shitty luck I've had with men—and my last encounter with Will back in January—I'm more convinced than ever life put the one for me right in the path of a bus.

It's been over seven months since I last saw Will. I avoid him every time I'm down here to see Paige. I think she caught on the last time we were hanging out. I faked food poisoning the second I saw Will walk into the bar we were at, and I was out the door before he ever knew I was there.

It hasn't been easy to avoid him, but I know it's what's best for my heart. I can't deny my attraction to Will, but I can avoid putting myself in a situation where he can jerk my heart around.

It's why I put off moving down to LA for so long. Paige has been trying to get me here for almost a year. I almost made the change back in January, but then decided distance between Will and me was in my best interest. The Gazette was a good job, and I excelled there. There was no solid reason to switch jobs at that point.

Over the summer, though, I decided enough was enough. I don't want a man to be the reason I don't move my career forward. Plus, I really missed being near Paige and my family. It was the best decision for me, and I refused to let Will stand in my way any longer.

But now that I'm actually moving here, the thought of having to interact with Will again causes nerves to flit throughout my belly. Hopefully I'm strong enough to finally resist the undeniable pull Will Edmonson has over me.

NINE

Will

I walked into the restaurant twenty minutes late due to traffic on the 405. I took in the scenery around me, the glow from the lights on the Christmas tree in the corner near the hostess stand, and the two guests sitting on a bench nearby waiting to be seated.

I walked over to the hostess. "Hi, I think my party is already here. It should be under Edmonson."

She checked the book in front of her and replied, "Yep, right this way."

I followed her toward the secluded corner where my sister Becka sat scowling at Candace. I couldn't see Candace's face from this angle, but it looked like she was talking and whatever she was saying was clearly pissing off my sister.

Fan-fucking-tastic.

This was not how this dinner was supposed to go. I really needed my sister on board here. Candace and I had been together for four months, although I'd been on the road for a lot of the time, or busy doing promos. But still. She's my girlfriend, and it would be really nice if my sister could respect that.

"Hey, ladies," I said when I got to the table, dropping a kiss to

Candace's cheek when she glanced up at me with a bright smile on her face.

I smiled back at her, a gentle warmth flowing through me. Candace looked at me differently than other women had, and I was still getting used to it. She didn't look at me with dollar signs in her eyes, which was a common problem amongst us NFL guys.

"Sorry I'm late. Traffic was a bitch. What have I missed?"

"Nothing much. Just Becka and I catching up. I think I'm going to go powder my nose before we order. I'll be back, baby," Candace said as she got up from her seat, her arm grazing over my shoulder before she walked away from the table.

I watched the sway of her hips, enjoying how her dress hugged what little curves she had. She was more endowed in the front, which I wasn't going to complain about, but I'd always been an ass man, so whenever she wore something tight, I was all over it.

I turned to my sister, bracing myself for what I knew was coming based on the facial expressions I'd seen on my way to the table.

"Did you pull out of a sponsorship deal because Candace told you to?"

Okay, that wasn't what I was expecting.

"No," I reply immediately, but then I remember the athleisure company that wanted to work with me. When Candace found out, she went on a rant about how terrible they were and said it would reflect poorly on us both if I represented them. So, I backed out of the deal.

"Well, okay, yes, there was one—" I don't get to finish my sentence before Becka cuts me off, her brows furrowed in confusion.

"Why would you let her dictate your career like that? Isn't that what your agent is supposed to help you with, not your girlfriend?"

She said the word girlfriend like there should be air quotes around it. I quickly looked toward the bathrooms to make sure Candace wasn't on her way back yet before leaning closer to my sister, determined to shut this down.

"Stop. Candace is a part of my life. She means a lot to me, and it would be really great if you could be even just a little bit supportive."

I sat back up just as Candace came into view. I locked my gaze on my sister, and my heart dropped at the disappointment in her eyes. Why couldn't my sister just give her a chance?

Becks crossed her arms and sat back in her chair, staring at me for a moment before whispering, "I would be supportive if I thought she was worth the support, but that woman has an agenda, Will, and I don't trust her. Please tell me you see it."

Her pleading tone threw me off, but before I could respond Candace arrived back at the table. I spent the rest of the evening feeling unsettled—Becka's words running through my mind and making me wonder why she couldn't just be happy for us.

My body hits the ground with a thud, my muscles screaming at me from the pressure of the linebacker still lying across me.

Fuck me, this game is kicking my ass.

"You okay, Edmonson?" I turn my head to see Matt has his hand outstretched to help me up. Now that the brick shithouse of a man isn't on me, I can finally catch my breath. I grab the offered hand and get up.

"Yeah. Fuck, I'm sick of getting tackled. These guys are all over me."

"You and coach gotta talk, because you going across the middle isn't working anymore, dude. You know it puts you at the most risk for getting hit, and you're just not making it happen out there like you used to."

I shake out my limbs and hustle to where my teammates are lining up preparing for the next play. Once upon a time, I was known for being one of the best receivers when it came to catching passes across the middle. It's a skill that proves a receiver's toughness, but this is only our first official game of the season and I'm already failing miserably. Probably because my head's not in the game.

My demons are catching up with me. I'm feeling pulled in a million directions, and if I don't deal with it, I'm going to break. But dealing with it means finally being honest about everything that went down the night Candace died. It also means coming to grips with the fact that Gina's avoidance of me these last eight months has been more painful than I'm ready to admit.

I shake my head, trying to refocus on the game in progress. The field is supposed to be where I excel. I need to prove I deserve to be here, because these days being an NFL player feels like the only thing going right in my life.

The game slogs on. I get tackled another half a dozen times before Jack starts passing to other receivers. It's a blow to my ego, but I know it's for the best. I'm not getting a damn thing done, and we have a game to win.

We barely scrape by, winning by only a field goal. The locker room is crowded, and guys are celebrating the victory, even if it was only by a small margin. At the end of the day, a win is a win.

"Edmonson!" I turn to my head coach, who's standing by the offensive coordinator.

"Yeah, coach?"

"My office."

Fuck, this can't be good.

I get up from the bench, ignoring the looks of worry from Jack and Matt. When I walk into Coach Denton's office, he points to the chair in front of his desk. His office is decent sized and covered in team paraphernalia. The only personal touch is the picture of him and his daughter Nikki hanging on the wall right next to his desk. Derek Peters, the offensive coordinator, stands next to Coach Denton's desk, while coach sits behind it. I take a seat and wait to find out why he's called me in here.

"Edmonson, what the hell is going on with you out there?"

I fight my body's desire to fidget by squeezing the arms of the chair until my knuckles are white.

"Sorry, Coach. I'll get my head in the game. Promise."

The coaches give each other a look, and my stomach drops. Derek looks back at me. "Will, you're one of the best receivers this team has ever had, but you haven't been the same the past couple of months. We gave you some slack when your game slipped after your fiancée died because we figured you were mourning, and it paid off because you came back focused and strong. But your game has been a mess since training this summer, and we can't ignore it anymore."

I interrupt before he can say more. "I know. I just need to get back in the groove. I'll be in top shape before the next game."

"I have my doubts about that, Will. To put it bluntly, you're playing worse than ever."

That's a blow I wasn't expecting. I know I've been a little off my game, but fuck.

Coach Denton folds his hands and leans on his desk. "Sorry, Edmonson, but we're putting you on second string until you show us you deserve to be back in a starting position."

My heart plummets.

I can't lose football. It's all I have left. And being demoted from a starting position is just a step toward being traded.

Fuck.

Candace has taken enough from me. I won't let her take this too. Time to face my fucking demons.

TEN

Gina

I pull up to the apartment in Burbank that is all mine for the next year. A major perk of moving down to LA was I was finally able to get a place of my own. No more roommates. Jack and Paige pull the U-Haul up behind me. My brothers wanted to help me move, but Paige and Jack were more than enough help. I didn't have much to move since most of the furniture belonged to my previous roommates. I'll definitely need to go shopping here soon so I can fully furnish my new place.

Paige runs over to me and grips my arms, shaking me back and forth with pure joy on her face. "I'm so excited that you officially live here!"

I laugh. "Me too. You have no idea how excited I am."

"It took you long enough to make the move." She looks at me knowingly.

I roll my eyes. I'm not going to respond to that. Instead, I look at Jack talking on the phone and standing near the back of the U-Haul.

"Jack's not going to be stuck on the phone with his agent, is he?"

"Uh...he's not on the phone with his agent." Paige shoots me a guilty look, which makes me nervous. What could she possibly feel guilty about?

"You're not about to move, are you?"

"No, we definitely aren't moving." She purses her lips and then her eyes look at something behind me. "Please don't be mad," she whispers.

My stomach drops. Please tell me she didn't.

"Hey, Gina. I heard you needed an extra pair of hands to move into your new place."

I close my eyes, clench my jaw, and attempt to take a deep calming breath. I could strangle Paige right now, but I won't because I love her and she's my best friend. I just need to really remind myself of that fact right now because I'm absolutely furious with her.

I turn around, and my heart beats frantically at the sight of Will. I can't stop my eyes from taking in his fit build. God, why does he have to look so good all the time?

Paige quietly excuses herself, snagging the keys to my apartment from me on her way to Jack.

Will and I stand there just staring at each other. He grips the back of his neck, having the good sense to look uncomfortable. This is the first time we've been face to face since Sugarfina. Seeing him makes my heart ache. I thought I was strong enough to finally be in the same city as him, but now I'm not so sure. I wish he didn't have so much power over my heart, or that time had diffused this intense chemistry that seems to always pulse between us.

Will takes a step closer. "It's been a long time," he speaks softly, a shy smile on his face but nerves clear in his gaze.

I look up at him, my walls firmly in place. "Not long enough," I whisper.

His face falls, and I'm surprised by the look of anguish that overtakes him. "Gina...I..."

"I need help with these boxes, Will. Paige is a weakling," Jack shouts from the U-Haul.

Paige slaps his arm. "I am not!"

Will glances back at them play fighting and grabbing at each other before turning back to me. "Gina, I'd really like—"

I cut him off, saying, "I appreciate the offer, Will, but it's not necessary. I don't need any more help. Jack and Paige were all I needed to pack up all my stuff. I'm sure it'll be fine with just the three of us. I'm sure you have better things to do with your time."

He's about to respond when I throw out sharply, "I don't need you."

He looks at me closely, his gaze locked on mine. His head drops, and he takes a breath before looking back at me with his deep emerald eyes. "Message received. Loud and clear. I didn't mean to interrupt."

His soft voice, piercing eyes, and the finality of his words threaten to penetrate the wall I've built against him. Right when I'm about to break, he steps back and turns to walk over to Jack.

I take a deep breath in an attempt to slow my furiously beating heart before turning to see Will giving Jack that man hug guys do. He says something in Jack's ear and then slaps him on the back before walking to his car. Jack watches him walk away and then looks back to me, confusion on his face.

"What did you say to him?"

"The truth," I say softly.

Except that's a lie. The truth is I told Will what I needed to in order to protect myself from getting hurt by him again.

So how come I feel worse than ever?

Paige walks over to me, a box in her arms. "Here, why don't you take this box up to your apartment. We'll be right behind you."

I quickly take the box from her and make my way to my new

one-bedroom apartment, attempting to rid myself of the remorse that is slowly seeping into my veins as I process my latest interaction with Will. When I get inside, I set the box down on the floor and look around the space. It's exactly like I remember it from a few weeks ago, and I'm already brimming with ideas for how to make it my own. I'm walking around my bedroom, getting ideas, when Paige comes in.

"I think I'll put the bed against the wall over there. That way I can put a nightstand on each side and still be able to see out the window."

"Why did you make Will leave?"

I sigh heavily. I should've known this was coming.

"Can we not? I'm tired from the drive, and I just want to get all settled in. I don't want to talk about Will."

"Too bad. I do. You think I don't know he's the reason you pushed your move? I almost had you convinced to move here back in January, but then suddenly when the team got back from their playoff game up there, you decided you were going to stick it out at the Gazette. Will was a fucking mess, and it wasn't because they lost the game. What the hell happened between you two?"

"Nothing," I huff.

"Bullshit."

"It's not bullshit," I yell. "Nothing fucking happened." I take a deep breath, feeling the fight leave my body as I relive that night. When I close my eyes and concentrate, I can still feel the heat of Will at my back and his erection pressing against me. I can hear his whispered words laced with desire, the same words that one moment were telling me he wanted me and the next claiming it was a mistake.

"Nothing happened, Paige," I practically whisper. I clear my throat and find my voice. "Something almost happened, but...but he said it was a mistake."

"Oh, Gina." Paige's sympathy nearly does me in, but I stay strong.

I shrug my shoulders. "He was probably right. Can you imagine the disaster we would be if we got together? I mean, I have practically the worst history with guys, and who the hell knows what his problem is."

"Why didn't you tell me?"

I look at her. "And admit to my best friend a guy I'd been crushing on for a year thought it was a huge mistake when he didn't even kiss me? Yeah, no thanks. I'd rather you not think I'm totally pitiful."

She steps closer to me. "I would never think that of you. I wish I had known. But I think he lied to you."

I move away, heading back to the living room, hoping I can distract myself by unpacking the box I carried up. "It doesn't matter."

She grabs my arm, stopping me. "It does." She turns me so I'm completely facing her. "Will was a mess when he got back from that playoff game. He's been off all summer. Jack said he's been playing like shit and even got benched because he was doing so poorly."

"Will got benched?" She nods. "That sucks, but it has nothing to do with me."

"I think it does. You remember the night you pretended to have food poisoning?"

Damn. I knew she was on to me, but this confirms it. I nod guiltily.

"Yeah, I knew, but that's not the point. Will showed up because I said you were going to be there. He wasn't planning on coming out. When he found out you'd left, he looked like someone had just stolen his puppy. He barely talked to anyone and ended up bailing after only an hour or so."

"That doesn't prove anything."

Paige groans. "Ugh, why do you have to be so fucking stubborn." She grips my arms and shakes me gently. "That man wants you."

I've had enough. "Then why does he constantly push me away? Huh? If he wants me so badly, why, at every possible opportunity, does he continue to shove me aside? He's toying with my emotions, and I can't take it anymore. I'm done, Paige. I was done in January. He had his chance and he fucked it up. A girl can only take so much rejection. Please, just let this go."

I walk outside and run into Jack right outside the door, a box at his feet. He looks at me with a sad, but guarded expression on his face.

"There's more to Will than you might think. It's not my story to tell, but I want to see my friend happy, and I think you might be the only one who can pull him out of the hole he's dug for himself."

My shoulders sag in defeat. "Jack, I wish that were true, but you can't pull someone out of a hole they don't want to get out of."

I walk down the stairs back to the cars, my heart and mind heavy, one part of me wishing Will and I could make it work, and the other wishing I'd never met him at all.

ELEVEN

Will

I stumbled in the door, throwing a parting wave to the guys as they drove off. We all needed to blow off some steam this week, me especially. I can't remember the last time I was this drunk, but it was easier to toss back four or five beers—or nine— instead of dealing with what's really been bothering me.

"Will? Where the fuck have you been?"

Speak of the devil.

"I was out with the guys," I mumbled as I made my way to the kitchen in search of water. I was going to have a killer headache tomorrow if I didn't drink a ton of water before I passed out.

"It would've been nice if you would've told me. I've been worried sick."

I wished I could believe her, but the longer we'd been together, the more I'd started to notice the cracks in her façade. A part of me still loved her, but now there was doubt festering in my veins. I could never quite put my finger on what it was, but our relationship didn't feel right. Not to mention the fact she'd caused a massive rift between my sister and me and didn't even seem to care.

"Since when do you worry about anyone but yourself?" I mumbled as I turned on the water from the kitchen sink and filled a tall glass.

Candace's fake concern evaporated, and her eyes flashed with ire. I was tired of playing this game with her. She was so hot and cold sometimes, and if I didn't love her so much I probably would've ended it months ago instead of letting it drag on for ten months.

"I don't think I can do this anymore," I whispered, leaning my hands on the counter facing away from her.

"Do what?"

I might have been drunk, but I didn't miss the hint of panic in her tone. I drank heartily from my glass before turning back to her.

I pointed between us. "This. You and Me. It's not working anymore, and you know it." The words caused an ache in my chest, but I couldn't ignore things anymore. My sister and I hadn't been on the best of terms in months, Candace was getting more and more demanding about having a say in my career choices, and I was tired of feeling torn all the time.

She stepped toward me, her face a perfect mask so I couldn't see how she was genuinely feeling.

"You don't mean that, Will. You're drunk. Come on, let's get you to bed. We can talk more in the morning."

Her tone was perfectly composed, which unsettled me. Shouldn't she be mad? Or upset? Something?!

I looked down on her, confusion in my eyes. "How are you not upset?"

She looked up at me and something in her eyes made my stomach curdle. Or it might have been the beer. But I think a large part of it was her. Her gaze was a mix of determination and something else I couldn't quite put my finger on in my inebriated *state, but I could tell it wasn't the normal emotion one would have when they're being broken up with.*

Her gaze softened, and her hands slid up my chest and around my neck. "Because I know you don't mean it," she whispered softly, her breath caressing my lips. She ran her fingers through the hair at the base of my skull causing shivers to race down my spine. My eyes closed of their own accord at how good it felt. My lids were heavy when I opened my eyes, and lust flooded me when she slid one of her hands down my pants against my quickly thickening cock.

"I know you want me, Will."

"What?" I whispered.

What were we even talking about? Fuck, her hand felt good. She grabbed my hand and took me to our bedroom. I briefly remembered I was supposed to be mad at her right now, that I was trying to break up with her because even though I loved her, something was off. But then she grabbed my dick again and stroked me until I was hard as steel and aching for release. Suddenly nothing mattered except getting lost in the heat between her thighs.

I leave my therapy appointment and head to a restaurant nearby. I'm emotionally worn out from talking about my shit for the last hour. I called Becka the second I got benched, and she recommended a psychologist for me to talk to. She said it was about damn time.

This was my third session with him in the past week, and while I feel like I'm starting to make progress, it's also bringing to the surface emotions I've long since buried—or mostly buried. The anger, resentment, betrayal, and guilt I rotated through after Candace died are now constantly simmering just below the surface. It's always a little worse right after a session, and I'm not even being completely honest with him yet. I think he can tell, but he has the decency not to say anything. It's not that I don't want to be, it's just I'm struggling to find the words.

After burying everything deep inside for the past three years, it's hard to expect it to just come rushing out right away. That's not how it works. At least that's how my psychologist, Dr. Stein, explained it. He's acknowledged it takes time for the pieces we hold deepest to work their way up, especially if we've been holding on to them for so long.

I make my way into one of my favorite restaurants in LA. It's a little fancier than I usually go for, and oftentimes is filled with couples, but the food there is worth being surrounded by people in love. I'll just have a nice meal and then be on my way.

The waitress seats me at a table tucked in a corner, so I can have privacy away from any prying eyes. I order an IPA and the house special and sit back and observe the people around me.

My heart stops when I see Gina being seated across from a man in a tailored suit. He's tall, but not as tall as I am. I can't see his profile from here, but I'm guessing he's decently attractive because Gina has a bright smile on her gorgeous face, her honey-brown eyes glowing in the soft lighting. I caress her cheek with my eyes, soaking in every line and curve.

She's clearly on a date. A first date by the looks of it.

He rests his hand on top of hers on the table, and I clench my jaw as heat moves through my veins. I'm taken aback by the fierce jealousy slamming into me. My gaze is locked on their clasped hands, until finally I look up at Gina's face, searching for some sign she is opposed to the touch.

On the contrary, a light blush is clear on her cheeks. My chest constricts, and a heaviness settles over my entire body. That should be me. I should be the man who puts a blush on her cheeks. She flashes him a soft smile, and the reality that I've really lost my chance overwhelms me.

The resentment that's been stirred up from my therapy session starts to simmer closer to the surface. Candace has taken so much from me. I've even let her take away the first woman I've felt anything for in years. Fuck that. Not anymore.

I think about how I tried to apologize when I came to Gina's new apartment. I tried to explain, but she wouldn't let me. She can't deny what's between us until she hears me out. I may not deserve the chance, but I'm going to beg for it nonetheless. These last eight months not seeing her or being near her have been more painful than I ever imagined, and now that we're in the same city and I'm working on getting my shit together, I can't stop myself from fighting for the opportunity to finally be with her.

I slowly rise from my seat and purposefully walk across the restaurant, my eyes locked on Gina. She's nodding her head at whatever Mr. Fitted Suit is saying when her eyes glance to the side and land on me. They widen before she takes a noticeable breath and pulls her hand from her date's. I smirk at the action.

I still have a chance.

Mr. Fitted Suit is still talking when I reach their table, but my eyes are locked on Gina's.

"And then the dealership said they could bump it up with all the best features for free since I'm such a well-known client." Arrogance drips from his lips with his words. Finally, he notices I'm there. "Oh! Hey, don't you play football for the Wolves? Holy shit, you're Will Edmonson. I'm a huge fan!"

Of course he is.

I fight the urge to roll my eyes. This is clearly a guy who's going to name drop this encounter for the rest of his life.

"Do you think I could get a selfie?"

I watch Gina carefully to gauge her reaction to her date's

request. Her gaze finally drops, and she fidgets with her hands in her lap. When she looks back up, she looks disappointed and maybe even a little embarrassed. I have no idea what she could possibly be embarrassed about, but I hate the self-doubt I see across her features.

I finally turn to her date and reply, "Sure." I paste a friendly smile on my face as he quickly gets up from his seat, pulling his phone out of his pocket at the same time. He swings his left arm up over my shoulder like we're buddies while he extends his right arm in front of us as far as he can. He takes a couple of pictures before looking down and examining them right in front of us.

This guy may have a tailored suit and expensive watch, but he has zero class. I'm curious how Gina got paired with him. I look back at her and notice she's glaring at Fitted Suit.

"Oliver," she says, trying to pull his gaze away from his phone screen.

He doesn't acknowledge her but instead turns to me, talking about how great he thought I did in the last game. Clearly this guy doesn't pay *that* much attention, since I was benched last game. I never saw any playing time.

"Oliver!" There's no missing the frustration vibrating through Gina's voice.

He looks at her, clearly annoyed she's interrupted his moment with a famous football player.

"Christ, what? Can't you see I'm busy?" He turns to me. "Some women, am I right?" He rolls his eyes like she means nothing.

Anger burns hot throughout my body, and it takes everything in me not to deck this guy for how disrespectful he's being to her.

Gina glares at Oliver before lifting her chin and straightening her shoulders. "I think we're done here. Thanks for the drink." She tosses back the rest of her drink and stands gracefully from her seat. She grabs her purse hanging from the back of her chair, nods at me, and then starts toward the door.

I give Oliver the briefest of glances and smirk at the shocked expression on his face. I'm guessing not many women have put him in his place. Pride swells inside me, and without another thought for Mr. Fitted Suit, I run back to my table, drop a hundred down, and then hustle after Gina.

TWELVE

Gina

I really thought this date would be different. He'd been so charming on the phone when we set up the dinner. I'd been hesitant to try online dating again, but decided to give it one more shot. Oliver was polite, handsome, and connected. That last factor didn't used to matter, but now that my best friend is marrying a famous football player, I've found people who already have connections to wealth or fame tend to be a little less fangirlish when they finally meet Jack and all his football friends.

So, imagine my embarrassment when Will appeared at our table and Oliver did just that. God, I can't believe he asked for a freaking selfie! To be fair, the date was going downhill before Will ever arrived. Oliver had boldly placed his hand over mine, which hadn't been so bad until he'd mentioned how he usually expected his dates to get manicures when they're going to get dressed up. My cheeks had flamed with embarrassment, and I'd tossed him a polite smile trying to shove away his cutting comment.

Now that I'm not around him, my embarrassment has turned into rage. I wish I could say what I think in the heat of the moment, but I've never been that type of person. Instead, I come up with the best comebacks when I've already left the situation. Usually when I'm at home, curled up on my couch, overanalyzing it.

My steps falter when I hear Will call my name. "Gina! Wait up!"

I slow my pace and take a deep breath, closing my eyes and preparing myself to be faced with the one man I know I should stay away from. Why did he have to be here? Why *this* restaurant? God, the moment I laid eyes on him, it was like no one else existed.

What is it about him that makes everyone else disappear? That makes me feel like I'm the only woman in the room? And why the hell can't we find a way to make that feeling last?

"Gina, are you okay?" His words are soft and low. He's careful to not draw attention to us.

I turn to face him, my heart in my throat as I trace my eyes over his firm jaw, soft lips, and then connect with his intensely brilliant green eyes.

Try as I might to keep my wall in place, I can't. I'm exhausted and burnt out from *another* disastrous date. It's left me feeling weak and vulnerable, two things I can't afford to feel around Will, the one man who could actually do significant damage to my heart and not just my pride.

"Gina?"

I let out a heavy exhale and then lock my eyes on his. "I can't do this with you tonight, Will."

"Do what?"

I swing my finger between the two of us. "This." Defeat fills my voice and my shoulders sag. "I don't have it in me to deal with your emotional whiplash tonight. I just don't." Something sparks in his eyes and his expression turns fierce. I try to ignore it. "I need to go. Goodnight, Will."

I go to turn around, but his hand reaches out and gently grips my arm right above my elbow. "Wait. Please," he pleads.

I turn back to him hesitantly. His eyes dart back and forth between mine, searching—for what, I'm not sure.

"I let you drive me away at your apartment, but I can't do that this time."

"I don't know what that means. Please, can we not do this right now?"

"Gina, I'm sorry about what happened in San Jose." I can hear the remorse in his tone, but it doesn't change the hurt I felt that night and for months afterward.

"It doesn't matter anymore," I dismiss it like it didn't kill me, even though it did.

"It does." He faces me straight on and slides his hands down my arms until he's holding my hands between us. I'm distracted by the warmth and comfort spreading through me at the contact.

"I never wanted to hurt you."

"You didn't," I say defiantly.

He looks at me like he knows I'm lying, but he doesn't call me out. That actually wins him points in his favor.

"I don't know how to do this very well. I haven't felt this way before."

I squint at him, doubtfully. "Paige told me it's been a long time since you've dated, but that you were in a pretty serious relationship."

"I was." He pauses. "But it was never like this with her."

That takes me aback. My blood pumps faster through my body, attempting to keep up with my now racing heart. "Like what?" We've never actually vocalized whatever this is between us.

"Like I can't breathe unless you're next to me," he whispers, and my heart catches in my throat. "Like my world is just this dim existence until you walk into the room and everything is suddenly covered in a bright light." He steps closer to me, our bodies just barely touching, and forces me to tilt my head to look up at him. "Like if I don't kiss you right now, I'll die."

Before I can respond, his hands cup my cheeks as he bends down and takes my lips with his own.

Fireworks explode across my eyelids as he deepens the kiss. My heart leaps with joy, and when his tongue dances with mine, my body melts against his. He lets out a soft groan, and I know without a doubt I can't fight this anymore. I grip his biceps, my fingernails digging into his coat as I hope and pray he won't pull the rug out from under me this time.

THIRTEEN

Will

Holy. Fuck.

This woman.

I can't stop the groan that slips out the moment our lips connect. Everything inside me settles, and for the first time in years my world feels right. Gina's lips part, and I gently coax her tongue to dance with mine. Her lips are lush, soft, and giving. God, I could kiss this woman forever.

Her fingernails dig into my arms through my jacket, and she leans into me. Her body fits perfectly against mine, and I'm overcome with how badly I need her. I can't believe I've been denying myself this moment for so long.

I'm a fucking idiot.

It nearly broke my heart when she looked at me and pleaded not to put her through any more emotional whiplash.

If my brief stint in therapy so far has taught me anything, it's that we often hurt those we care about the most when we deny our own issues. Gina's plea confirmed I'd done just that with her, and I hate myself for putting her through that. Kissing her seemed like the only way to prove to her I was done fighting.

And now that I've kissed her, I have no intention of going backward. This woman is mine. Whether I deserve her or not.

But I have to do this right. Gina deserves the best, and fuck knows she's way out of my league, but I want to give her everything.

I reluctantly slow down our kiss and pull away. Her eyes slowly blink open. She looks dazed, and I love that I put that look in her eyes. Suddenly, her soft gaze turns apprehensive.

"Do you regret it?" she whispers.

My heart clenches. Fuck, I've really messed things up if her first thought after our kiss is that I might regret it. Shit.

I shake my head. "Not for a second."

Her shoulders sag with relief, and I realize I have a lot of work to do to prove I can be the man she deserves.

"I want to take you out on a proper date."

She looks at me in shock. "What?"

I smile softly at her, tucking a lock of hair behind her ear. "You heard me. I want to take you out on a date."

"You're sure?"

"I've never been more sure of anything in my life."

She tries to fight her smile but fails, and I catch the blush that heats her cheeks. I brush the back of my hand against her cheek and then delicately cup her chin and bring her mouth back to mine.

I want to live in this moment forever. Never in the history of the world has a woman's mouth fit so perfectly with a man's. I'm convinced our lips were made for each other.

For the briefest moment, I realize this woman is going to own me in a way no one ever has. The thought slides quickly from my mind when her fingers curl into the hair at the back of my neck.

God, that feels good. It's been so long since anyone's touched me like this.

She kisses me deeper and lets out the sexiest little moan. My blood rushes south, and that's when I know I need to slow things down. I don't want Gina just for sex.

Don't get me wrong, I plan to fuck the hell out of this woman. But I want so much more with her, and after all I've put her through, I need to prove myself to her.

I pull away. "Okay, I'm going to need you to stop, or else I'm going to take you right here."

She smirks. "Would that be such a bad thing?"

Ugh, I'm going to have the worst case of blue balls tonight.

"Yes, because then other people might see you, and I have no intention of sharing you with anyone else."

Her look turns heated, and when she licks her lips, I'm certain she's doing it just to torture me.

"Where are you parked?"

She points to a car just a few feet away. I place my hand against the small of her back and walk her to her car.

When she opens her door, I give her one more quick kiss and then take a step back. "A proper date. Tomorrow night. I'll pick you up at seven."

She watches me closely for a couple of seconds before nodding.

Relief floods me, and all my muscles release the anxious tension I wasn't even aware I was holding. "Okay. I need to go now before I take this too far tonight."

Her flirty smile tells me she understands what she's doing to me. "If you must. I'll see you tomorrow."

She gets in her car, and I watch as she drives away. I let my head fall back as I look up at the night sky, feeling my body relax in a way it hasn't in years. Gina is a game changer, and one I'm done pushing away.

FOURTEEN

Gina

"Tell me again about the kiss." I roll my eyes at the giddiness in Paige's tone as I put her on speakerphone so I can finish getting ready. How she has the ability to combine giddiness with a hint of know-it-all, I'll never know.

"I already told you everything there is to know about it."

"God, I'm so excited for you guys! I knew you two would be perfect for each other if you'd just get out of your own way. You have to be the two most stubborn and difficult people I've ever met."

I hold a figure-hugging black dress against my chest, looking in the mirror.

"I don't think this dress is sexy enough. I look like a nun, despite how this dress would hug my curves."

"Try the deep crimson dress. You never wear it, but it makes you look smokin' hot."

I look in the mirror one last time, pursing my lips. "Yeah, maybe you're right."

"What do you think changed?"

I shuffle hangers while I dig around to find my red dress. "What do you mean?"

"I mean, you said he seemed different when you kissed, and he wasn't standoffish afterward like he has been. What do you think changed?"

"I don't know. Has Jack said anything to you about Will?"

"Not since he told me about Will getting benched. But maybe that has something to do with it. I'm sure sitting there watching the games has given him a lot of time to think."

"Maybe."

"You sound nervous."

"I'm not." I am.

"You're lying."

"I'm not, I swear." I am. I really am.

I don't know that I've ever been so nervous about a date. Maybe when I was fifteen and went on my first date ever with Trevor Thompson. He came to pick me up, and my dad answered the door with a shotgun along with my three brothers behind him all holding baseball bats. Poor Trevor. I wasn't the least bit surprised when he never talked to me again.

Tonight, my nerves have nothing to do with my family intimidating my date. Tonight, they're about who I'm actually going on a date with. I wish I could understand what's changed for Will. If I close my eyes, I can still feel his lips pressed against mine. I just hope I don't get the old bait and switch tonight. My brain has put Will into two categories—Hot Will and Cold Will, his very own version of Jekyll and Hyde, basically. Hot Will makes my heart flutter and tingles spread throughout my body. Cold Will makes me want to rip my hair out and cry. I've had enough of Cold Will ruining whatever is happening between us.

"I don't believe you."

Of course she doesn't. Because she knows me. "You could at least pretend, you know."

She laughs. "Yeah, right. That's not the kind of friend I am, and you know it. If you want someone who will lie to you all you have to do is look in the mirror."

God, ain't that the truth. "Harsh, Paige."

"But true. Have you put on your dress yet or what? Text me a picture!"

"Calm your tits. It's been ages since I've worn this dress. I hope it even still fits." I pull it off the hanger and slip into it, impressed my ever-expanding hips haven't made this an impossible feat. The older I get, the more I understand my mother's jokes about getting wider with age.

I pull the back zipper all the way up and then turn around to face my reflection in the mirror.

Woah.

"Well? I'm dying over here, Gina. How's it look?"

"I look hot," I say, somewhat surprised. I don't remember looking this good the last time I wore this dress.

"Send me a picture!" Paige demands excitedly.

I swear, I don't know who's more excited for this date, her or me. I send her a picture and wait for her response.

"Holy shit!" she gasps. "You're going to bring this man to his knees!"

I smile seductively at my reflection. "I'm sure I can find something for him to do while he's down there."

"You're terrible," she laughs. "But seriously, Gina. You look absolutely gorgeous. I wish I could see the expression on Will's face when he sees you."

I glide my hands down the soft, deep crimson fabric and glance at the clock. Nerves flood through me when I see I only have ten minutes before he'll be here. I swipe on some dark red lipstick to match my dress, slip on my shoes, and then reach for my clutch. Just as I'm transferring over my debit card and driver's license, there's a knock at my door.

"He's here. I'll call you later."

"Have fun!" Paige hangs up and leaves me to face Will all on my own.

I look into the hallway mirror next to my coat closet. "Okay, you've got this. You are a strong, confident woman, and even if he flips the switch and turns into Cold Will, you will survive. Go and have fun. You can do this." I nod my head at my reflection, determination fierce in my eyes, and head for the door.

FIFTEEN

Will

I'm more nervous than I expected to be as I knock on Gina's door. I've been looking forward to this date all damn day.

Nerves tingle down my spine. Fuck, what if my breath stinks? I cup my hand over my mouth and blow, inhaling the minty freshness of my breath, my shoulders sagging in relief. I seriously don't think I've been this anxious about a date in my entire life.

I hear the handle on the door rattle and lock my gaze on where Gina should be standing. Nothing could've prepared me for the sight before me when she opens the door. I practically swallow my tongue as my eyes slide from her black stilettos up her toned legs to the hem of a dark red dress that sits mid-thigh and hugs around her hips in a way that makes me jealous of an article of clothing. I follow the hourglass curve of her body up to the bodice of her dress, where I have to fight back a groan at the cleavage which is practically being served to me on a platter from her sweetheart neckline. There's about an inch of fabric going up to her shoulders and wrapping around her neck. When she turns around to close and lock her door, her back is bared to me, and I look up to the ceiling praying I don't come in my pants before we even make it to the restaurant.

She turns back to me, and her honey-colored eyes hold me hostage. Her makeup is natural and not overdone, but her pillowy lips are a deep crimson that matches her dress and invites all kinds of filthy images to my mind.

She looks so goddamn sexy.

She's a fucking goddess, and I want to worship her for as long as she'll let me.

"Ready to go?" she asks.

I clear my throat and turn my body away, hoping she can't see the evidence of my desire. I can't even form words right now; my mind is a pile of mush. I simply gesture toward the entrance of her building and follow her like a puppy dog.

When we get to the door, I rush in front of her so I can open it for her. She smiles up at me, and my heart stutters in my chest. I follow her out and place my hand against the small of her back to guide her to my car. The second my hand touches the bare skin of Gina's back, heat ignites in my gut. I hear her inhale sharply and fight every instinct I have telling me to take this woman right here, right now.

How is it possible our chemistry seems to be getting even *more* intense?

Without a word, I open the passenger side door of my Mercedes. When I close the door, I slowly walk around to the driver's side, taking my time so I can try to compose myself before I'm trapped in a confined space with a woman who brings all my desires to life.

It's a wasted effort.

The second I start the car, her perfume wraps around me and I'm convinced this is going to be the longest night of my life.

I'm impressed when we make it to the restaurant without me crashing the car. I asked Gina how she was liking it at Newsworthy, and fortunately she carried the conversation during the drive.

The restaurant is a quaint little French bistro type place Jack recommended. I haven't been on a date in over three years and had no idea where to take Gina tonight. I didn't have enough time to make a reservation somewhere fancier, but based on the smile that lights up Gina's face when she sees where we are, I assume this was a good call.

"I love this place! Paige and I have come here a couple of times for a girls' night. The food is amazing."

I place my hand on her back and lead her through the doors to the hostess stand. "You'll have to tell me what's good."

"You've never been here?" She looks surprised when I shake my head.

The hostess leads us to our table, and once we're settled into our chairs, Gina looks at me curiously. "What made you pick this place if you've never been here before?"

I slide my hands up and down my thighs. "Jack recommended it." I watch her closely hoping this doesn't work against me.

I'm relieved when I catch a soft smile on her face before she looks down at her menu. "I'm glad you took his recommendation. I think this might be one of my favorite restaurants in LA."

She looks up and our eyes lock. Tension pings between us, nearly tangible with its intensity. I clear my throat and try to think of how to steer us away from anything that will make me think about sex.

I look over my menu. "So, what do you recommend?"

"The duck is to die for, but the chicken tagine is also delicious." We peruse the menu for a few minutes, talking about the different selections. When the waitress comes over, we place our orders—the duck for her, the chicken for me.

"So, Paige mentioned your family lives down here. Are they excited to have you living closer?"

She laughs. "Oh yeah. Although I forgot about the added pressure that comes with living close to family. My mother has already started hassling me about getting married and having babies." She rolls her eyes and shakes her head.

An image of Gina with a rounded baby belly slams into me, and want floods through me. Fuck, I bet she'd be gorgeous pregnant.

Where the hell did that thought come from?

I shake the idea from my mind. "Do you have any siblings?"

She nods. "I do. I have three brothers, two older and one younger. And I also have an older sister."

"Wow, I bet things were never boring in your house."

She chuckles. "They definitely weren't. Do you have any siblings?"

"Yeah, three sisters. We were raised by a single mom, so I was the man of the house."

"Are you the oldest?"

I shake my head. "No. That honor goes to Lainey. I'm the next oldest, then Becka, and finally Elise."

"You know, I can't believe this hasn't come up before, but I just realized I don't even know where you're from."

"I'm from Texas. I grew up outside of Austin."

"And do your mom and sisters still live there?"

"My mom and Elise do. I bought my mom a new house in Austin about a year ago, and Elise decided to stay there with her so she wouldn't be by herself."

She places her hand on her chest. "You bought your mom a house?" When I nod, she gushes, "Oh my God, that's the sweetest thing I've ever heard."

I shake my head, embarrassed by her praise. "It was honestly the least I could do. My mom is the best, and we certainly weren't easy kids to raise. She deserves so much more than I could ever give her."

Gina looks at me with such admiration, I start to shift in my chair, uncomfortable with the unfamiliar yet unspoken praise. A blush stains my cheeks, and I take a drink of water in an attempt to hide it. She catches on to my evasive maneuver.

"So, where do Lainey and Becka live?"

"Lainey lives in Laguna Beach, working with a startup company down there. Becks lives in Santa Monica, working for a streaming service in their PR department."

"Becks?"

"Sorry, yeah, it's my nickname for Becka. We've always been really close. We're only eleven months apart. It feels more natural to call her Becks than Becka. How about your siblings? Do they live close by?"

"My family is spread around Southern California mostly. I was the only one who flew the nest and left the state to live in Chicago for a while."

"In college, right?"

"Yeah. My oldest brother, Luis, lives in Long Beach near my parents with his wife, Mia, and their two boys, Sebastian and Adrian. My other older brother, Diego, lives in Santa Ana with his wife, Amanda, and their three kids."

"Three?"

"Yep, two girls, Alondra and Gabriela, and a boy, Carlos. Those girls have Diego wrapped around their little fingers. It's adorable."

I smile at the affection in her voice.

She continues, "My older sister, Marisol, lives in Huntington Beach with her husband, Derek, and their six-month-old baby boy, Alex. And then finally, my baby brother, Andres, lives in San Diego."

"Is he married?"

She barks out a laugh. "Um, definitely not. He is an absolute playboy. I'm pretty sure he's slept with half the girls at UCSD by now. He has no desire to settle down any time soon."

"And your parents?"

"They live in Long Beach in the same house I grew up in."

"Are you close to them?"

She plays with her wine glass. "Yes, but it wasn't always easy growing up in such a big family. On top of all my siblings, we constantly had friends and family coming through our house. It was hard to stand out in that kind of environment. I struggled to find my fit. It's probably what drove me to go to Chicago for college. I wanted to find out who I was away from my family."

"Did you?"

She looks at me from across the table, the tea candle flickering a soft glow on her delicate face. "For the most part. There's always room for improvement."

I reach out and gently clasp her hand in my own. "I know exactly what you mean. Even when we feel like we've got our shit together, there's always room for growth."

Her gaze locks on mine, and something passes silently between us. An acknowledgement of all the mistakes we've made on this path to each other, and hope we can put those mistakes behind us and really give this thing a shot. I stroke my thumb over the top of her hand, relishing this moment with her. Her dark hair falls softly around her shoulders, and I itch to slide my fingers through it and tug while I bury myself inside her.

We spend the rest of the date swapping stories about our siblings. When the check comes, I'm not ready for the night to end, but I'm in this for the long haul with Gina and I want her to be sure of us before we take that step.

The ride back to her apartment goes by too quickly, both of

us filling the car ride with more anecdotes about our families or our childhood. I pull up to her apartment building, park, and then walk around to open the car door for her. When she gets out of the car, I reach my hand out, and she slides her delicate fingers through mine and continues to hold my hand until we make it to her door. She turns to me when she pulls out her keys.

"Do you want to come in for a drink?"

Yes. Without a doubt. But if I go in there for a drink, I won't leave until after I've buried myself inside her and made her come at least a handful of times. I've managed to restrain myself throughout this whole evening, despite how fucking stunning she's looked all night. I know better than to test my restraint any further.

"I think I should probably head home."

She looks down, but I don't miss the disappointment covering her face.

I tilt her chin up with my finger. "I'd really like to take you out again."

Surprise lights her eyes. "You would?"

"Yeah. I'm going out of town for a game and have some promo stuff this week, but how about next week?"

"Next week sounds good."

I smile. "Great."

Gina smiles back at me, and I can't resist her any longer. I step closer and slide my hand through her hair, simultaneously pulling her closer to me. Her smile drops, her mouth parting as her gaze heats and darts between my eyes and lips. I lean my head down and just barely brush my lips against hers. Her mouth is just as soft and lush as I remembered. With a groan, I press my mouth on hers, taking her in a searing kiss I wish would never end. Her hands grip my hips, while her lips mold to mine.

We get lost in each other for longer than I intend, but I don't regret it for a second. Her mouth is fucking perfect, and I want more of her. She moans and melts into me, her body fitting perfectly against mine.

A door closes down the hall, jarring me out of my reverie. We look at each other, eyes glazed with lust.

"Are you sure you can't come in?" She speaks softly like she's afraid she'll ruin the moment.

"I can't. If I come in, I won't stop at just kissing you."

"Would that be such a bad thing?" she asks huskily.

I groan, then give her one more soft kiss before I step back. "I want more than just your body, Gina. I've been a dick for the past two years, and I don't want you thinking I only want sex with you."

"What do you want?"

"Everything," I whisper. This is the first time I've truly been vulnerable with her. She could absolutely reject me right now, and I wouldn't even blame her after how much of an asshole I've been.

"I'm not going to sleep with you until I'm convinced you know I'm in this. All the way. This isn't just a passing whim for me. I want you. All of you."

She stands before me, clearly stunned if her wide eyes are any indication.

"I'll text you, and we can figure out a plan for our next date."

"You don't have my number."

I grip the back of my neck, nervous about how she'll take this. "Actually, I do. I got it from Jack about six months ago."

"Six months ago! But you've never texted or called me."

I nod. "I know. I got it because I wanted to apologize about what happened at Sugarfina."

"What did happen that night?"

"That's an explanation for another night. Right now, I have to go before I ravage you in this hallway. I wish you could see what I see when I look at you. You're fucking gorgeous, and I'm having a really hard time walking away."

"I've already said you don't have to go."

"Yes, I do. I have a lot to prove, starting now. I'll talk to you soon. Night, Gina."

"Goodnight, Will."

I thought these past three years were hard, but tonight proved me wrong. Nothing has been harder than leaving Gina outside her door, her eyes filled with lust and need.

I'm a man on a mission. I will prove to her I deserve her, no matter what it takes, even if it means dealing with the worst case of blue balls in the history of the world.

SIXTEEN

Gina

For the past week, Will has made good on his promise to text me. He's texted at least once a day asking me how my day was going, and we've even started talking on the phone at night until both of us are too tired to continue the conversation. I can only continue to hope this means Cold Will is gone for good. If this week is any indication, Will definitely has no intention of giving me the brush-off.

My phone buzzes against the restaurant table, pulling my attention from Paige's story about the new puppy they just got. When I grab it, it vibrates against my palm, and the screen lights up with a text message from Will.

Will: I can't wait to see you tomorrow.

"I lost you, didn't I?"

I look up to Paige, smiling at me and shaking her head. "What?" I ask.

"I'm guessing by the smile on your face Will just texted you."

I blush. "Maybe."

"And what is the fine William up to today?"

"He's at the dog park with Rex and his sister."

"Has he told you yet what you two are doing for your date tomorrow?" she asks as she takes a bite of her house salad.

"No. He just told me to dress comfortably and bring a jacket."

She shakes her head. "Don't men understand we need to know how to dress appropriately for the occasion? Men have it so easy—sweats, jeans, or slacks. Women have a million options."

I laugh around the bite of my club sandwich and nod in agreement, which is all Paige needs to continue her mini rant.

"Seriously though. I hate when Jack tries to do that surprise date thing unless he tells me exactly what I should wear."

I shrug. "Well, he did say we'd be outside, but occasionally indoors so to wear layers. That was helpful at least."

"Men."

"Can't live with them," I say.

"Can't live without them," she finishes. "At least we can train them."

We break into laughter and enjoy the rest of our girls' night.

A smile breaks out on my face when Will parks near the Santa Monica Pier. Memories come flooding back of the visits I made here as a child with my siblings.

"It's been ages since I've been here."

"Is this a good surprise?"

"The best. It's like being a kid again," I reply as I smile at him.

He smiles wide, and I notice a slight dimple in his right cheek. *Damn, he's sexy.*

"Prepare to get your ass handed to you in the ring toss though. I don't mess around when it comes to winning jumbo stuffed animals," I challenge him.

He laughs, and the sound shoots desire straight to my core. I don't think I've ever seen him be so carefree.

Will slides his fingers through mine as we walk toward the pier and watch the street performers around us. There are people breakdancing, performing magic tricks, and singing.

"Aren't you worried about getting noticed?"

He shakes his head. "No, not really. I've come here a few times with my sister, and I rarely get hassled. A couple of people might ask for autographs or a picture, but it's not too bad. I think most people are used to seeing celebrities around here, so it doesn't faze them the same way it does in other places."

"Does it ever bother you?"

"Which part?"

"Any of it. I know Paige has talked about how some people will walk up to Jack and act like they know him simply because they see him on TV. She said people even come up and touch him like they have some right to him. I think that would drive me crazy."

He shrugs. "It's all part of the job. It's definitely not my favorite, but I just tend to brush it off. I'm not the quarterback, so I get that kinda thing a lot less than Jack does. Not to say it doesn't happen, because it does. Just not as frequently, so it's easier for me to ignore."

"Did you always know you wanted to play football?"

"Yeah. Football is a big deal in Texas. It's the equivalent of hockey in Canada. Everyone in Texas plays football, and if they don't then they go to all the games and know all about it. It's like a rite of passage."

"When did you start playing?"

He scratches his jaw. "Fuck, I think I was maybe ten the first time I played in a junior league. I was a little young, but my coach saw my talent even then, so they fudged some things so I could play. I was surrounded by girls at home, so it was a nice escape. My coach ended up being a stand-in dad for me. He's a good guy. We still keep in touch."

I smile at the fondness in his tone. "That's cute."

"What about you? Did you always want to be a reporter?"

I shake my head. "No. When I first went to college in Chicago, I had no idea what I wanted to be. Then, my sophomore year I took a journalism class to fulfill an elective credit and fell in love with it."

"What do you love most about it?"

I think for a moment, trying to organize my thoughts to best explain what I love about my job. "I love the hunt of a good story. I like finding out information and sharing it with the world. I'm sure a psychologist would say that stems from my family life. I was always hunting for secrets my brothers and sister were trying to hide and then tattling on them."

He laughs. "I'm sure that made you popular."

"Oh yeah," I say with a smile. "Although, Marisol definitely didn't appreciate it when I found out she'd been sneaking her boyfriend into her room in the middle of the night. She paid me fifty dollars to keep her secret."

"Did you?"

I nod. "Yeah. I always looked up to Mari. If it had been my brothers, I probably would've taken the money and tattled anyway."

He laughs. "That's savage. I'm glad my sisters never did anything like that."

"I'm sure they thought about it."

"I'm sure they did."

We approach the opening for Pacific Park, and Will buys our tickets. "So, what first? Games or rides?"

"Hmm, well, I guess that depends. Are you ready to have your ass handed to you by a girl, or do you want to build up to it?"

He laughs, and I see his dimple again. "Come on, smart-ass. Why don't you put your money where your mouth is? Let's play some games, and whoever loses the most buys the winner dinner."

"Deal."

Will shakes his head at me, the jumbo bear hanging from his back, the paws held firmly in his hands like it's riding piggyback. "I can't believe you won me a bear. Isn't that supposed to be my job? I'm feeling a little emasculated right now."

"Toughen up, buttercup. This is a woman's world, and you men are just living in it."

He laughs and shakes his head at me. "Alright, so since you schooled me in all these games, what do you want for dinner?"

"Mmm, how about corn dogs?"

"You don't want to go somewhere fancier?"

"You can't come to a place like this and eat fancy food. This is carnival food. Corn dogs, French fries, all the fried doughy goodness of elephant ears."

"As you wish, m'lady."

My heart stutters. "A *Princess Bride* reference?"

His eyes practically twinkle, and I damn near melt at the endearing expression on his face. "I grew up with sisters, remember."

"Then you should know what that phrase really meant to Wesley."

His eyes connect with mine. "I do."

Two simple words, and my heart stops in my chest before restarting at a rapid pace. I can't even think of a response to his comment, but I can't break eye contact either. The longer we stare at each other the more the tension builds between us, until I'm convinced it has to be a tangible thing everyone on this pier could see if they looked closely enough.

I finally break eye contact, my senses returning to me. "So... corn dogs. I thought I saw a stand back that way." I turn in that direction and start walking, hoping he follows me.

He does.

The tension fades as we eat our corn dogs and fries while drinking lemonade. It is a perfect afternoon.

"Want to go on the Ferris wheel?"

I grin like a little kid. "Definitely."

The sun starts to fade into the ocean as we make our way to the line for the Ferris wheel. There's something about this time of day that feels calming and romantic, despite the crowd and chaos of the games around us.

The ride operator allows Will to leave his jumbo teddy near him, and we make our way into our seats. Will shakes hands with the operator while whispering something to him. When he sits next to me, I ask, "What was that about?"

"Just thanking him for watching my bear. My girl won me a prize. I don't want anyone to snatch it while we're up here."

My girl. Swoon.

The ride starts up, the swinging motion making my stomach flutter like it always does, although this time I suspect the flutter has more to do with the man sitting next to me than the ride itself.

"You cold?" he asks.

A shiver skates across my arms. "A little."

He wraps his arm around me and pulls me close to his body. "Better?"

Oh yeah. "Yeah, thanks."

I look up at him, his sandalwood scent surrounding me. Our eyes connect, and his gaze holds me hostage. Slowly, oh so slowly, Will leans down and our lips meet. The kiss starts soft, but within moments, the pressure in my chest feels immense and my longing for him overwhelming. His right arm holds my body closer to his while his left hand grips my cheek. He deepens the kiss on a groan, and everything around us disappears as I get lost in this kiss. Our lips mold together in a dance of harmony, our tongues sliding delicately against each other.

The Ferris wheel jolts, rocking our seats and causing us to break our lips apart. Our eyes open and lock on each other once again. My breath feels heavy as I stare at Will and see my desire reflected in his eyes.

I want this man with every breath in my body.

He slides his fingers through my hair, watching the movement in fascination before looking back at me.

Without another word, his lips slam against mine and his mouth owns me. This is something else. This kiss is heat, passion, need, and hunger. He growls low in his throat when I meet his intensity with my own.

Time stops.

The world disappears.

All that exists is the two of us, becoming one.

It is easily the most sexual encounter I've had that wasn't actually sex. No man has ever owned me with a kiss like Will does.

I'm not sure how much time passes before our seats start rocking as the Ferris wheel begins moving again. I don't really care either. All I care about is the man next to me. The man who is quickly embedding himself in my heart in a way no other has.

As terrifying as the thought is, especially with our history, I don't want it to stop.

Jesus, take the wheel, because I'm about to hop in the back seat.

SEVENTEEN

Will

I grip my shaft as the hot water slides down my body, the image of Gina's eyes on the Ferris wheel spurring me on. The familiar tingle signaling I'm close shoots down my spine. I tighten my grip and speed up my rhythm, fantasizing about what could've happened if we had taken our kiss further. The picture of Gina licking her lips with that hungry look in her eyes tips me over the edge, and I shoot my release against the shower wall.

Tension releases from my body like a waterfall, starting at my shoulders and making its way down my torso and finally my legs. I extend my arm and place my hand against the wall to catch myself from my overpowering release, a shiver going down my spine while my head hangs down under the showerhead.

Fuck, I needed that.

I've been fighting blue balls for days. I deserve a medal for dropping Gina off at her door with a kiss goodnight instead of fucking her against the wall like I wanted.

Fuck, that woman does something to me.

I park in front of Gina's apartment and sprint up the stairs. I may be a little eager to see her. When she opens the door, my jaw drops.

"Goddamn. Way to make it hard on a guy."

"That was the point," she says with a sly smile, her eyes caressing my body as she takes in my loose muscle tank and basketball shorts. While she checks me over, I do my own perusal, fighting the urge to slide my hands and tongue across every inch of her gorgeous body. She's wearing tight booty spandex shorts which show off her delectable ass and a loose tank top that leaves most of her midriff exposed. She looks fucking droolworthy.

I will not fuck this woman yet. I am strong enough to resist her.

God, please let me be strong enough.

With that final thought, I gesture to my car, words still stuck in my throat at how sexy she looks. She tosses me a knowing smile as she walks past me, clearly aware of how she's torturing me.

"If this is payback for me not coming in after our date a couple of days ago, you win."

She laughs.

We make small talk on the drive to Griffith Park. It's the middle of the week, so it shouldn't be too crowded. I don't even bother coming here on weekends. I'd be hounded by tourists wanting a picture or autograph.

We pull into the parking lot, which is busy but not full, indicating we should be in the clear with the crowds.

I grab the backpack I packed with a blanket and our lunch. Gina grabs a couple of water bottles out of the back and puts them in the side pockets of the backpack and then we make our way in. The plan is to hike some of the trails and then have a picnic.

It's still pretty warm for October, so it doesn't take long for each of us to work up a sweat. After about a half hour of hiking, Gina stops for a drink of water. I'm about to sip my own when I see her drip some down her front and rub it in. The water mixed with the glistening sweat on her body makes my blood heat.

She catches me staring. "You know, it helps if you actually put the bottle to your lips."

I stare at the bottle in my hand, realizing I've just been standing there with it suspended right in front of my mouth. "Oh, is that how it works? Damn, I've been doing it wrong all this time. How did I ever survive without you?"

She smirks. "Beats the hell out of me."

"You're very distracting, you know."

"Am I?" She just winks at me. The minx. She knows exactly what she's doing to me. "So, we've covered jobs and family. What should we discuss on today's date? Exes?"

My stomach clenches. "No, I don't think we're at exes yet."

For a moment, I question my decision to stop going to therapy. I've been doing so well, and my game has picked up, not to mention how well things have been going with Gina. Coach Denton has me starting again, so I didn't feel it was necessary to keep going. But my reaction to Gina's suggestion makes me wonder if maybe I quit prematurely.

I brush the thought aside. I'm fine. It's fine. I'm just not ready to explain Candace to Gina. That's all this is.

Really.

"So, if you don't want to talk exes, then what secrets are you willing to reveal to me today?"

"Secrets, huh?"

"Yep," she replies, popping the p.

"What kind of secrets do you want to know?" I'm a little worried she might ask about Candace. I don't know if Paige has mentioned anything, but I know she knows a little bit about my past because Jack told me. I hold my breath waiting for Gina's response.

"What's the story with your dad?"

I exhale. Not my favorite topic, but it's a whole hell of a lot safer than Candace.

"That's a long story."

"Seems we have a lot of time while we hike around."

"Alright then." I motion for us to keep moving while I talk. "My dad bailed on us when I was five. Just old enough to remember the dickhead."

"Why'd he leave?"

"Because he was a selfish prick. He decided he wasn't cut out to be a father, which he wasn't wrong about, but leaving my mom to raise four kids by herself was a dick move."

"God, I can't even imagine how hard that was."

"Yeah. Lainey and I tried to help my mom as much as we could. Becks and Elise were still too little to fully understand what was going on. It was hard for a long time. My mom had to get a second job just so we could make ends meet. It was rough."

"Have you talked to your dad since he left?"

I nod. "Once. He reached out to me when I got drafted by the Wolves."

"No way."

"Yep. He just wanted his fifteen minutes of fame. He didn't care about me. Fuck, he didn't even ask about my mom or sisters. He just wanted in on my football fame. He wanted to be seen with me. He's a real piece of work. I told him if he ever came near me or my family, I'd drag his name through the media and make sure his fifteen minutes of fame showed the true story of what a shithead he was. He was apparently dating a woman who was the CEO for a big cell phone company at the time and couldn't risk losing his meal ticket, so he backed off."

"What a cockroach." Gina scoffs.

"Yep. That's exactly what he is."

She places her hand on my arm, stopping me. "I'm sorry you had to go through that, Will."

Her kindness and empathy weaken my knees. I've had to be the tough guy for so long, it feels nice to have someone worry about me. Someone who cares about me who isn't related to me. Someone whose concern isn't a manipulation.

"It made me a better person. I'd never be that kind of father."

"I have no doubt."

"So, now we've uncovered that lovely piece of history. Any skeletons in your closet?"

She looks up to the sky and purses her lips, thinking about it. "I shoplifted once."

I was not expecting that. "What?"

"Yeah, it was technically an accident, but I've been banned from going into a JCPenney store ever again."

"How do you accidentally shoplift?"

"I was there with a bunch of girlfriends in high school, and we were looking at the makeup selection and suddenly I heard a voice behind me ask how I was doing. When I turned around it was Jon Miller, who I'd had a crush on since the fourth grade. I about melted into the floor when I saw him. I mean, he was the cutest boy in our school, and I didn't think he even knew who I was, but apparently, he did. He asked if I wanted to grab an Orange Julius in the food court, and I just nodded and started following him. It wasn't until security stopped me that I realized I still had the lipstick I'd been looking at in my hand. I tried to explain, but apparently they have a really strict policy about theft."

"How'd Jon take it?"

She covers her face. "Oh my God, it was so embarrassing. He totally bailed on me. He was there one second and then once security kept hassling me and asking me questions, he disappeared."

"What a douchebag."

She nods. "That's when my crush officially ended. I always felt he should've stood up for me or at the very least hung around to see it was completely unintentional." She shrugs. "Oh well, his loss."

"Definitely his loss."

She smiles at me.

"I would've fallen all over myself to get you to notice me in high school."

She laughs at me. "You would not!"

"I would have. I can just picture how cute you were. I bet you were beautiful even then."

Her cheeks deepen with a rosy blush. I brush my thumb across them, and her eyes close at the caress. I lean toward her and inhale her vanilla scent. There's a glisten of sweat on her body, but you wouldn't know it based on how she smells. I bend my head down to hers and drop a kiss on the top of her head.

When I pull away, she slowly opens her eyes and looks at me, her emotions written all over her face. It's not as noticeable as it used to be, but I can still see a little bit of fear in her eyes that tells me she still doesn't quite trust I'm going to stick around this time.

Seeing that firms up my resolve. I step back, knowing it's still too soon to let us go all the way. We're getting there, though.

Progress is still moving in the right direction, no matter how long it takes to get there.

The rest of our date is lighter. We eat our picnic, telling stories about how we were in high school and laughing at how dumb we were as kids. By the time I drop her back off at her apartment, I'm feeling lighter than air.

"You want to come in?" she asks.

"I don't know that I should. You still don't trust me yet."

"I trust you."

"Not all the way."

She chews her bottom lip but doesn't dispute it. I move closer to her, my thumb pulling on her lip until it pops free from her teeth.

"Don't doubt for a second how desperate I am to have you, but when you give yourself to me, I want it to be completely. I want to know you trust that I'm not going anywhere."

Her light brown eyes brighten at the sincerity in my voice. "Okay," she whispers.

"Okay."

I kiss her, letting her feel all my desire in my kiss, and then walk away, hoping she'll trust me soon.

EIGHTEEN

Gina

It's been over three weeks since our first date, and I'm hornier than ever. I've masturbated a disturbing amount of times this week—to the point where I wore out the batteries on BOB. What's even worse is the batteries died right before I was about to hit the big O. Talk about frustrating!

I tuck a lock of hair behind my ear and glance next to me at Will sitting in the driver's seat. He's been out of town for a game and then promotional meetings this past week. He said he was dying to see me but wasn't sure he could manage anything too exciting. I suggested a movie, and now here we are.

My eyes take in his disheveled black hair that looks like he's been running his hand through it. It's distractingly sexy, but nowhere near as sexy as his eyes. His emerald-green gaze is mesmerizing, and every time he looks at me, I just want to get lost in his eyes.

His body is equally distracting, especially tonight. He's wearing a fitted black T-shirt that hugs his biceps and hints at the abs he has hiding underneath. Or at least the abs I think are underneath. I tried to convince him to send me a topless pic when we were texting one night, but he refused on the grounds he'd want one in return and he didn't think he could take seeing me topless.

It's a relief to know he's being tortured just as bad as I am.

Will parks the car and comes around to open my door—always the gentleman. He buys our tickets and then we stand in line at concessions.

"So, what'll it be?" he asks, looking at the menu on the back wall.

"Well, popcorn, obviously."

"Obviously," he agrees.

"And Milk Duds."

"Why Milk Duds?"

"Because you put them in the popcorn, and they get all warm and melty. It's delicious. It's the perfect salty sweet combo."

"Huh, I've never heard of that."

I grip his arm. "Are you serious right now?"

He shrugs. "Yeah. I mean, it's usually a big deal if I get butter on the popcorn. I eat pretty clean so I can stay in shape during the season."

"While that makes sense, it's an absolute travesty you've never eaten the magic that is warm popcorn and Milk Duds. We are definitely remedying that tonight."

He smiles at me. "If you insist."

"I do."

When we finally get our popcorn and Milk Duds, he watches me with amusement as I poor a handful in our giant bin of buttered popcorn.

"You don't use the whole box?"

"I do, but if you pour it all in now, then you'll end up eating all the Milk Duds before the popcorn is gone. This way, it's spread out more evenly."

"Uh-huh."

Will probably thinks I'm nuts right now, but I don't mess around when it comes to my movie popcorn and candy.

We find our seats in the back, and it's not long before the lights go down and the previews start. I love the previews. I won't even stay for a movie if I don't get to see the previews. They're part of the experience. It's what makes seeing a movie in the theater stand out from just watching a movie at your house.

When the lights go out completely, I tip the popcorn to Will, offering him some. He takes a few kernels and pops them in his mouth. I shake the container insisting he take more. He chuckles at me and grabs a bigger handful. When I smile happily, he just shakes his head at me, a giant smile on his face.

I grab a few kernels and a Milk Dud and pop it in my mouth. The moan that comes out quietly is unintentional, but damn, this is delicious, and something I haven't treated myself to in months. I glance at Will about to offer him more popcorn, but the words get lost in my throat at the expression on his face.

He leans toward me, moving his mouth to my ear to whisper, but instead of leaving distance, his lips graze against my ear, warm air blowing gently on my skin and causing goose bumps to pepper my neck and arms. "Do you have any idea how fucking sexy you are?"

I turn my head, our eyes connecting. I want to reply, but I can't think of anything except how good his lips look right now. He lets out a low growl and then grips the back of my neck and brings my mouth forcefully to his. The roughness of his touch and his tongue working against mine is so insanely hot I might actually combust in this movie theater.

He takes the bucket of popcorn and places it on the floor between us. My now empty hands search in the dim lighting for his legs. I want to feel him.

I'm desperate to feel him.

My fingers slide up the dark wash denim, and my breath whooshes out of my body when I feel his erection—a steel bar is more like it.

Holy moly.

When I put pressure into my touch, he lets out a low groan against my neck.

"Gina."

It's a plea—for me to stop or for me to keep going, I can't tell. But I know what I want to do. Without waiting another second, I undo the button on his jeans and slide down the zipper. He tips his head back, his eyes closed and his breathing labored. I slide my hand under the band of his boxer briefs. My small hand barely touches the velvety steel of his erection before he lets out another groan and turns into me.

"Shh," I whisper laugh.

"Fuck, Gina," he breathes out.

Watching this giant powerhouse of a football player be completely defenseless against me is a huge turn-on. I can't wait to see what he's like when I get on my knees for him.

And I will definitely be getting on my knees for him. If women think giving a man blowjobs makes them weak, then they aren't doing it right. Being on your knees in front of a man is when you ultimately have the most power over them. You have their greatest treasure in your hands and mouth. You own them.

I wrap my fingers around him, wishing I had bigger hands since my fingers don't even touch my thumb due to his girth. I only get a few pumps before his breathing gets erratic and he shoves my hand away.

He whispers against my hair, "If you pump me one more time, I'm going to come, and there's no way I can walk out of here with a cum spot on my pants."

Disappointment seeps through me. "I want you to come."

"I know. But not like this. Not where someone can snap a picture and make this very magical fucking moment something seedy and dirty," he explains quietly.

Oh.

I hadn't thought about that.

"Okay."

I'm still disappointed but try to brush it off. I go to reach for the bucket of popcorn, but Will gently grabs my hand to stop me.

"What are you doing?" he whispers.

"What does it look like? I'm going to eat more popcorn and watch the rest of the movie," I whisper back.

"I don't think so."

"What?"

"Just because I can't come, doesn't mean you can't."

Oh.

Ohhh.

Oh. Fuck. Yes.

With a salacious grin, he slides his hand up my exposed leg. I've never been so grateful to have worn a dress than I am in this moment.

His fingers are whisper soft against my skin, gliding up smoothly until they connect with that spot at the apex of my thighs. I'm glad he's not planning on teasing me too much tonight because I don't think I could take it. Not after the last three weeks of building sexual tension every time we see each other.

"Fuck, you're so wet already."

"I liked touching you," I whisper out on a breath.

He groans quietly in response and then moves my underwear aside and slides a finger inside me, his thumb rubbing circles on my clit.

I grip the armrests of the chair and bite my lip to keep

myself from screaming out. I have never had a man find my clit so quickly. Holy shit. It's like Will has a road map to my erogenous zones.

He pumps his finger in and out quickly, not messing around. I'm thankful we're sitting in the back in a mostly empty movie theater or this might be embarrassing.

Who am I kidding? It wouldn't have stopped me for a second. When you have a man as sexy as Will *finally* stick his fingers inside you, you just say yes.

Yes, yes, yes.

Oh, God.

So, so good.

In a matter of minutes, I come all over Will's fingers while biting my fist to keep from shouting out.

Relief flows through my body as all the tension I've been holding onto dissipates.

Wow.

Like *really* wow.

My body melts like jelly against the chair as I continue to come down from an exceptional orgasm. Without lifting my head from the back of the chair where it's resting, I turn to look at Will and see his ridiculously smug grin.

"Proud of yourself?" I whisper.

He nods and his grin gets wider.

Whatever. He earned it. I won't tease him about it.

I couldn't tell you what the movie was about. After the orgasm, we cuddle and I soak in every perfect moment of being in Will's arms, and finally start to believe Cold Will is really gone for good.

NINETEEN

Will

I'm beginning to hate my schedule.

It's been a week since I've seen Gina, and I'm chomping at the bit to touch her again. I've fantasized about her endlessly since our movie date. The chemistry between us has always been strong, but it was fucking explosive that night. I don't know how we didn't end up having sex when I dropped her off.

I seriously deserve a medal.

I pull up to her apartment and hop out of my car, eager to see her again. Phone calls and texts just don't quite cut it. Not when the alternative is getting to touch her smooth skin and taste her perfect lips.

She answers the door wearing snug dark-wash skinny jeans with a blood-red top which accentuates her cleavage, making me desperate to taste those lush breasts. A black leather jacket finishes her ensemble. Her dark hair cascades in soft waves past her shoulders, and I itch to run my fingers through it.

"Hey, handsome."

"You really need to stop dressing to torture me."

She laughs, grabs her purse, and closes the door behind her.

When she steps toward me, I pull her against my body and drop a kiss on her rosy lips. Her fingers grip my shirt, and she moans into my mouth. This. This is everything I can't get over the phone, and everything I've come to crave from her.

After only a moment, Gina reluctantly pulls away. "We should probably get going before I decide to forget about the concert and just take you inside my apartment right now."

It takes everything in me to resist this woman, but I do. With her soft petite hand in mine, we walk to my car.

"So, this band we're seeing tonight—you never told me who it was."

"Have you heard of Rapturous Intent?"

She stops and stares at me. "You're joking, right? Of course I've heard of them! They're the hottest rock band out there right now. Their songs are killing it on the Billboard charts."

I tug her hand gently to get her moving again so we don't miss the concert.

"Well, I went to high school with the lead singer. Despite our different interests, we were pretty close friends because we also lived on the same block and had similar upbringings. We've stayed friends, and he hooked me up with VIP passes for tonight."

"Shut up!"

I laugh. "I'm dead serious."

Gina grabs my arm and shrieks, "Oh my God. Oh my God! This is the best date ever. I promise I won't totally fangirl when we get there if you let me get it all out now."

"Do what you gotta do. Although I'm pretty sure Trent will gladly let you fangirl all over him."

"You'd be fine with me fangirling over another guy?" she asks skeptically.

"I'd rather you fangirl over me if I'm given the choice."

Her eyes soften, and she leans over to kiss my cheek. "I'm

going to do a whole hell of a lot more than fangirl over you, William."

Oh, fuck.

I open her door for her and then walk around the back of my car, discreetly adjusting myself to hide the effect her words have on me.

Gina spends the car ride gushing about how excited she is. She's been dying to see this band live but didn't get tickets in time. I'm feeling pretty fantastic that I'm the guy who is giving her something she's so excited about.

The VIP passes allow us to park in a special lot and go through a different entrance than most of the concertgoers. We arrive early and head to the VIP room, where we should be able to see the band either before or after the show, maybe both.

Before we make it to the room, though, I see Trent in the hallway about to head into his dressing room.

"Trent!"

He lifts his head and smiles wide when he sees me. "Will! Damn, man, it's good to see you!"

We give each other a guy hug —you know, the one where you pat each other on the back with one arm.

"It's good to see you too, man. This is my girlfriend, Gina."

Gina's head turns sharply to me, her eyes questioning. I guess we haven't used that term yet, but I figure that's what we are. I just look at her, hoping she can see I'm really in this. If the last month hasn't proven that to her, then I'm not sure what will.

Her eyes light up and she smiles softly before turning back to Trent. When he smiles at her, her smile widens.

"H...Hi." She giggles and I have to fight to keep myself from laughing at how she's totally fangirling right now, despite her protests in the car that she'd be able to keep it together around the guys.

Trent pulls her into a hug. "Any girl of Will's is a friend of mine. Nice to meet you. It's been a long time since Will's had a girlfriend, so you must be someone special."

Gina giggles nervously, and I snort out a laugh at her reaction. This is a new side to her, and I find it hilarious.

I look around at the chaos happening backstage and look at Trent. "You really did it."

Pride emanates from him. "Yeah. Some days I can't believe this is my life. But I bet you know how that is."

"Yeah, I can definitely relate."

"I'd love to catch a game next time we're in town."

"I'll hook you up. Just text me."

"Will do. You two gonna be around after? I gotta finish up my preshow ritual, but I'd love to catch up more."

I look to Gina who is staring at Trent—eyes wide, jaw open —in shock. I chuckle and then answer for the both of us. "Yeah, we'll be here."

Trent looks at Gina and then back at me, whispering conspiratorially, "I get that a lot. Don't worry, I won't steal your girl."

I pull Gina closer to me. "I'd fight for her, so you wouldn't stand a chance."

He smiles, a silent understanding passing between us. He knew about Candace—well, some things about Candace. He doesn't know it all, no one does, but he knows enough to understand the significance of me calling Gina my girlfriend. Without another word, he pats me on the back and then heads to his dressing room.

I bend down to kiss the top of Gina's head, grateful to be here with her. And even more thankful I finally stopped letting my past get in the way of us. That I stopped letting Candace get in the way.

"You gonna make it?"

"That was Trent Bridger."

"Yep."

"I just met Trent Bridger, and I *did not* play it cool."

I chuckle. "No, you didn't, but I think he'll forgive you. Come on, let's go check out the VIP room and then find our spot to watch the show."

The bass pumps from the speakers, making my heart thump heavily in my chest. Gina's body sways against me as she dances to the music, her back nestled against my front. The warmth in the stadium has steadily increased as more bodies gyrate to the music. I watch in fascination as Gina's skin begins to glisten from the higher temperature.

My fingers slide over her neck, and she leans her head to the side, giving me more access.

The band switches to a ballad, and the soulful, needy vibe matches my feelings perfectly, as I stare at this beautiful woman and wonder if I'll ever truly deserve her.

Gina leans her back against my front, and the gentle sway of her body against my dick causes blood to rush south, my thoughts going with it.

My hands glide down her smooth arms and then to her curvy hips. I love everything about her body—and the way her breath hitches when I touch her, how her lush ass nestles perfectly against my cock, how her scent always draws me closer. My thumbs graze the edge of her shirt, causing it to ride up. The feel of her soft exposed skin heats my veins, and need pummels me.

I want this woman more than I want my next breath.

When she rubs her ass against me, my dick goes completely hard.

I drop my head, burying my nose in her hair. I love how she

always smells like vanilla. Maybe it's my sweet tooth, but the scent makes me want to devour her.

It's probably just her.

She has this power over me no woman has ever had.

For the briefest moment, a memory of Candace using her body to manipulate me—something I didn't see until it was too late—niggles in the back of my brain, and my body stiffens slightly.

Gina turns her head toward me, her eyes meeting mine, and I push the memory aside. Gina is not Candace.

She's *nothing* like Candace.

I bend my head, my lips grazing her ear and then down farther to her neck. I kiss and suck, knowing I'll probably leave a mark but not caring.

I want to mark her as mine.

My hands slide up and graze the sides of her breasts while I continue to kiss her neck.

Her arm comes up and around, sliding into my hair, gripping the strands and tugging. I think I hear her moan, but the music is too loud to be sure.

God, I want to get her out of here. I want her in my bed, underneath me, writhing with pleasure. I'm thirty seconds away from taking her right here when she suddenly turns around and locks her eyes on mine. When I see her lust-filled gaze, I know I can't say no to this woman anymore.

She gets on her tiptoes, and I lean down so I can hear her over the music.

"Take me home."

I pull back, taking in her expression. "What about the rest of the concert?"

She shakes her head. "Take me home, or I'm going to go down on you right here."

Oh.

Fuck, that picture is hot.

But she's right. We can't do that here.

Without another thought, I grab her hand firmly in mine, and we push through the crowd making our way to the exit. I remember we're supposed to meet up with Trent after the show and decide I'll text him later. He'll understand.

When we make it out to the car, I shove her against the passenger door and take her mouth with mine in a kiss that leaves my body shaking as my hunger for her nearly overpowers me.

This woman owns me.

Body and soul.

She moans against my mouth, our tongues ravaging each other, and the sound is music to my ears. Better than any concert.

She breaks the kiss, breathing heavily. "I mean it, Will. Take me home. I'm done waiting. I want you."

"No more waiting." I struggle to think with all my blood in my dick.

The ride to my house is a blur.

My body hums with desire, especially when Gina continues to rub her hand over the bulge in my pants. As soon as the car is parked in my garage, we throw our doors open and meet in front of the car, our mouths crashing together as yearning consumes us.

Without parting our lips, I ungracefully move us through the door and into my house. We crash against the hallway wall, Gina rubbing her body on me like a cat in heat. My body burns for her.

We break our mouths apart long enough to rip each other's clothes off as we work our way to my bedroom.

I grip Gina's fine ass and lift, her legs wrapping around my hips instantly.

"Fuck, condom."

"Hurry," she says between planting kisses on my neck.

I carry her over to the bed and drop her down, then reach over to the nightstand and grab a condom. I'm thankful I bought a box when I was out the other day.

Placing it on the edge of the bed, I gaze in awe at the vision of Gina naked and writhing before me.

Nothing has ever been hotter than this right here.

I lift her left leg, kissing her ankle and switching between kisses, sucks, and licks as I make my way up to her knee.

Then her thigh.

All the way to where her thigh meets her already glistening pussy.

She squirms as I get closer to where she wants me most.

She groans in frustration when I drop her left leg and repeat my actions on the right. Her breathing is heavy and her moans are loud by the time I work all the way up her right leg.

"Will, please."

"Please what?"

"Fuck me."

"Mmm, I don't think so."

Her head shoots up. "What?"

"I want to taste you first."

I glide my fingers over her slick core, my cock harder than a fucking rock.

"I've been dying to taste this pussy."

"Fuck, you have a dirty mouth."

I grin at her. "You have no idea, Sugar."

And then I dive in.

Oh. Sweet. Jesus.

Her pussy is divine.

I slide my tongue up, listening to her whimpers turn to moans when I reach her clit. I suck it into my mouth as I slide a finger inside her wet heat. Fuck, she's tight. I'm going to need to work her up to my size.

I slip another finger in as I suck and lick her clit. She clenches around me, milking my fingers exactly how I want her to milk my cock.

"Will," she moans, and my need for her becomes overwhelming.

But I have no intention of stopping my ministrations until she comes all over my fingers and my mouth. I want to taste her release.

I lift my head. "Come for me, Gina."

"Oh God. Feels so good." Her voice shakes and her fingers grip my hair as her hips buck against my mouth.

Fuck, yes.

This is what I want.

I pump my fingers vigorously, hitting that magical spot inside her, and suck her clit hard.

She comes screaming my name and gripping my hair so hard, I'm convinced she's going to pull it out.

There's nothing hotter than watching a woman come, but Gina takes it up a notch.

She's divine. A sexual goddess. I could watch her forever.

Before her tremors have stopped, I pull my fingers away and slide the condom over my painfully hard erection. She's still coming down from her orgasm when I slide inside of her. Both of us moan in bliss at finally being connected.

"Fuck, Gina. You're so goddamn tight."

"You feel so good," she breathes out, her head tilted back, eyes closed.

"Look at me."

She opens her eyes slowly, and the desire burning in them sets me off. I pound into her going as deep as I can.

Fuck, she feels so damn good. I want her more than I've ever wanted anything or anyone. More than football, more than air.

I feel that familiar tingle shooting down my spine and straight to my balls. I'm not going to last long.

But damn, I wish I could fuck her all night.

She's so tight and wet. Her pussy feels like it was made for me.

That thought sets me off, and like a caveman, I relentlessly buck into her, wanting to own her body the way she owns mine.

"Oh God! I'm coming again!"

"Give it to me, Sugar. Milk my cock with that tight pussy."

"Will!" she screams as her orgasm takes her over.

She clenches around me and squeezes so hard I think I might black out from how good the viselike grip feels.

With one more pump, I come, letting out a deep groan and reveling in my release. I can't recall a single time in my life when sex felt this good.

After a minute, I roll to the side so I won't crush Gina with my weight, since I'm unable to hold myself up anymore. My body feels like jelly.

I turn my head to Gina.

Her eyes are closed, but she has a content smile on her face. Her lips are red and swollen from our rough kisses, and her body glistens with sweat from the intensity of our sex.

I roll to my side and slide my thumb across her cheek.

Her eyes open and her gaze locks with mine.

My heart pumps in my chest, contentment and need flowing through me. Need for her. Need for this to work out. Need for my demons to stay buried.

No words are said, but we both acknowledge with our eyes

that we're in this. There's no going back now. We belong to each other.

She cups my cheek with her hand, gazing softly at my face. I close my eyes at her soft touch and sigh softly, embracing the happiness I haven't felt in a very long time.

TWENTY

Gina

I wake slowly, the bright light of the room telling me I've slept in later than I normally do. My body is deliciously sore, muscles aching I didn't even know I had.

I stretch my arms over my head and arch my back before falling back into the plush heaven of Will's bed. I turn my head and watch Will sleep, a satisfied smile on my face as I look at the man who has made me feel more than I ever imagined.

He's lying on his stomach, his arms around his head and his hair a disheveled mess from all the times I gripped it last night. His toned back is on display for me, and I ache to run my fingers down the contours of his muscles, but I restrain myself because I'm sure he's exhausted.

We didn't get much sleep last night.

After our first round of sex, we dozed for a bit before I woke up with Will curled around my back and his erection pressing into my ass. That led to round two, which lasted longer than any sexual experience I've ever had.

That man's stamina is record-breaking.

A soft sigh escapes me.

I close my eyes, relishing this moment and how gloriously perfect everything feels right now.

Unfortunately, my body won't let me relish for too long. My need to use the bathroom comes on suddenly. I get out of bed and throw on a shirt sitting rumpled on top of Will's dresser and make my way to the en suite bathroom. When I come out, Will is still sound asleep. Instead of waking him, I head to the kitchen in search of some water.

There's a trail of our clothes from Will's room to the door connecting to the garage. A smile breaks out on my face as I remember how ravenous we were for each other last night.

God, that man is delicious.

My feet are soft on the cream tiled floors of his kitchen. I grab a glass and fill it up with the fridge water. Once it's full, I lean forward, my elbows resting against the counter, and take in Will's house. We kind of bypassed the tour last night, more eager to explore each other than our surroundings.

His house is a contemporary open concept with all newer model appliances. It's surprisingly clean for a guy. The only decorations are pictures of his sisters and a woman I'm guessing is his mom. There's a picture of his dog, Rex, and it suddenly occurs to me I haven't seen Rex the entire time I've been here. I look into the living room and see some dog toys lying around but no actual dog.

Arms wrap around my waist, and I lean back into Will as he nuzzles my neck, inhaling his scent and allowing the warmth of his body to wash over me.

"Mmm, why weren't you in bed with me?"

"I had to pee, and I got thirsty."

He kisses my neck and mumbles his words, "Unacceptable. I wanted to wake up next to you and see if we could break our record from last night."

My body turns to jelly. He's talking about my orgasm

record. I had five during our second round. The most I've ever had before Will was two.

Have I mentioned this man is a beast in the bedroom?

"I don't know if my body could handle more just yet."

"Are you sore?"

I don't miss the concern in his voice, and my heart melts a little more.

"A little."

"I can run you a hot bath if you want. I have a Jacuzzi tub. I've never used it, but I'm sure it would help."

This man.

God, what is he doing to me?

I'm fucking putty in his hands, that's what.

"A bath sounds heavenly."

"I'll get it started." He kisses my neck one more time and moves to go back to his room. I grab his arm, stopping him.

He looks at me. "Everything okay?"

I'm not quite ready to voice the question lingering in my mind, so instead I ask, "Where's Rex?"

Will eyes me closely. "He's at Becka's place. I had her take him since I didn't know how late we'd be out and didn't want him home alone." He pauses, then says slowly, "Was that really what you wanted to know?"

I take a deep breath, trying to calm my heart rate and steady my nerves. "How do you feel about last night?"

He looks at me carefully, clearly trying to figure out what I'm getting at.

I thought all my fears about Cold Will had disappeared, but waking up this morning, I realized there was a little nugget of worry that he might regret last night.

"Last night was more than I ever imagined. If I'm honest, it was the best sex I've ever had."

I smile wide at his remark.

"How was it for you?" he asks.

"The best I've ever had," I say softly.

He smiles. "Good. Now let me go make you a bath so we can do it again."

After a long soak in Will's amazing Jacuzzi tub, he makes good on his promise, and I'm pretty sure I discover heaven when he obliterates his previous record and I come until my body is completely wrung out.

Eight.

Eight orgasms.

Seriously? Who does that?

Will Edmonson, that's who.

Is this real life?

TWENTY-ONE

Will

I slide my finger up Gina's bare calf, her body wrapped in a sheet as she props herself on her elbow, her head resting in her hand.

She has a birthmark on the inside of her thigh that fascinates me.

"What are you thinking?" she whispers.

"I'm thinking I'd like to kiss this birthmark again," I say while circling said birthmark. "But if I do, then I'm just going to want to bury my head in your pussy again too."

"Anyone ever tell you that you have a filthy mouth?"

I smirk. "You like it, don't deny it."

"I do like it, more than I ever thought I would."

"You've never dirty talked in the bedroom?"

She shrugs. "Not really. Most of my sexual encounters were about ten minutes or less."

I sit up. "Seriously?"

She nods.

I lean back down on my elbow, my fingers continuing to explore her body. "That's a goddamn travesty. You should be worshipped. Your body is fucking heaven."

She shrugs again, but I notice her demeanor has changed.

"Tell me about them."

"About who?"

"These guys who didn't know how to pleasure you."

"You can't be serious."

"I'm totally serious."

"You want to have the ex conversation right now? While we're still naked?" she asks.

"Why not? I'm not intimidated by any of your exes. Not after you've already confessed I'm the best you've ever had. That's really all a guy needs to hear to know he doesn't have any competition."

She shakes her head. "You're ridiculous. Fine. If you must know, they've all been assholes."

I'd already figured that part out. I mean, only a dumbass would let a woman like Gina go. I should know—I was one for a while there.

"Go on."

"Do you want to hear about all of them or just the most significant ones?"

"How many are there?"

"I've had five serious boyfriends."

I absorb her words, realizing what she's telling me is she's had sex with more than five guys. That doesn't really bother me. Fuck knows I've had sex with way more than five women.

"Tell me about those. I don't need to know about the ones that weren't relationships."

"Okay, well, there was Michael in high school. He was my first boyfriend, and we dated for four months, but he kept lying to me about where he was going and started acting really sketchy."

"Was he cheating?" I ask.

She shakes her head, her hands caressing my arm while she

talks. "No, it turned out he had started selling drugs. I found out through a friend and broke up with him. I didn't want to be involved in anything like that."

"Yeah, that's bad news."

"Yeah. My second boyfriend was Nick, my senior year of high school. I thought we were unbreakable. He treated me well, was respectful to my parents, and even became friends with my brothers."

"So, what happened?"

"I finally had sex with him, and he broke up with me the next day."

"What the fuck?!"

"Yeah, but the shittiest part was when he told me he only dated me to win a bet. I was a virgin, and I guess it was obvious because a bunch of guys decided to make bets on who could deflower a virgin before the end of the year. Once I found out, I was beyond heartbroken. I couldn't understand why he would go to all the trouble just to win a stupid bet."

I slide my hand up to her cheek, my thumb grazing it gently.

"I'm so sorry you had to go through that."

She shrugs and brushes it off. I've seen my sisters date some losers, but nothing quite like that. They've had their hearts broken, so I recognize the pain she's reliving.

"I understandably took some time off from dating and didn't date anyone until my junior year of college. His name was Collin." She sighs heavily before continuing, "We were together for almost two years and were even living together our senior year. I thought we were going to get engaged, but then I came home and caught him fucking his TA in our bed. Her moans tipped me off, but I didn't want to believe it until I opened the door and saw them with my own eyes. I broke up with him and moved in with Paige for the last couple of months of senior year. He followed me to San Francisco when I moved there and has tried to convince me to give him another chance multiple times, but the image of that girl riding him is burned in my brain, and I think I'd probably throw up if he even tried to kiss me again.

"You know, the first time we met, I actually only drove down to LA because Collin kept trying to get ahold of me and wanted me to give him another chance. I was tired of dealing with him, so I decided to get away for the weekend and come visit Paige."

My body heats at the idea of this guy trying to win her back.

Fuck that.

He had his chance. She's mine now.

I pull her toward me, so her head rests on my chest while she tells me about the next two idiots who fucked up their chances with her.

"After Collin, I casually dated, but San Fran guys aren't great, at least not the ones I've found. I dated a DJ for three months, but his career and schmoozing people for connections was his priority. I fell low on his list and didn't like that. I wanted to be with someone who wanted to be with me, not someone who treated me like I was convenient. My most recent relationship was with Andrew."

"When was that?"

She pauses while she thinks about it. "Wow, almost a year and a half ago now, I think."

I think about the timeline in my head. She must've dated him after the club event where she overheard me tell Max I wasn't interested in her. I can't believe all the time we've wasted because I couldn't pull my head out of my ass. Because I let Candace haunt me and control my life. A different kind of guilt than what I normally carry pulses through me.

"What happened with him?"

"He cheated too. With his secretary. Original, right?" She scoffs. "We were only together a few months, but it still hurt."

"They were fucking idiots. You know that, right?"

"Yeah, now. But at the time it just hurt to be treated like I meant so little to them."

I kiss her head, holding her tighter. I wish I could take away all her hurt, but then she probably wouldn't be here with me if it weren't for her history.

"What about you?" she asks. She tilts her head up, looking me in the eyes.

I can't look at her while I tell her about Candace, so I look away, focusing on the ceiling.

"I've only had one significant relationship."

"One?" There's no denying the shock in her voice.

"Yeah. I didn't really date in high school. I was too busy with football and working a job so I could help my mom with the bills. I dated and messed around with girls, but never had an official girlfriend. In college, I was focused on football and maintaining my scholarship, so it was much the same as high school. When I got drafted, I was pumped. My coach warned me against jersey chasers who try to trap a guy while he's on his way up, so I cooled it with my meaningless hookups. With my upbringing, I was always hyperaware I didn't want to live away from my kids if I had any. So the idea of being trapped by a woman with a baby was even less appealing." I barely cover the disdain from my voice, trying not to give more away than I'm ready for.

She nods. "I bet."

I take a deep breath before continuing on. "My rookie year, I met Candace. She was the daughter of an important businessman, so I knew she didn't need money or connections. She was energetic and always the life of the party. Whenever she walked into a room, all eyes were glued to her. She lived off the attention. I couldn't help but fall for her."

"What happened?" Gina whispers.

"We dated for almost a year before I proposed."

She looks at me sharply. "You were engaged?"

I pause. I figured Paige would've told her, but apparently not.

"Yeah. I thought you knew."

"No. I didn't know."

Without another word, she lays her head back down on my chest, her hand resting on my stomach. I wrap my arm around her tighter, hoping she can feel how much she means to me. I don't want her to get the wrong idea about Candace and me, but I can't tell her the full story.

"Keep going," she whispers.

I hesitate, unsure if she means that or if she is just saying it. Even with all my practice with my sisters, I am not always good at reading women. Do I keep going?

She looks at me. "Will, tell me what happened."

"We got engaged and things changed. Our relationship wasn't the same as when we first got together, and she even hid a drinking problem from me."

This is where I should tell her everything. The door is wide open.

Instead of walking through it, I slam it shut.

"She died in a car accident. Drunk driver," I whisper the last two words, barely able to get them out.

Gina looks at me, tears in her eyes. "Oh my God, Will. I'm so sorry."

I pull her head back down to rest on my chest hoping she can't see the remorse in my eyes.

Some days I'm glad she died. After everything she put me through, all her lies, her betrayal. But my guilt always overrides the relief that I never have to see her again.

After all, I killed her.

TWENTY-TWO

Gina

I'm still reliving my conversation with Will about our exes, even four days later. I can't believe Paige never told me he was engaged. I ripped her a new one for that.

I mean, girl code, HELLO!

She could've told me that much at least.

She did apologize for not telling me, but Jack had sworn her to secrecy. I guess I can forgive her, even though I felt completely blindsided at the time.

My heart aches thinking about Will's voice when he told me he'd been engaged. He must've really loved her something fierce to propose to her when she was his first serious relationship.

I can't help but wonder how I compare to Candace. Especially for a man who held out on having a serious relationship as long as he did. Is he still in love with her?

He's called me his girlfriend, but that would only make me the second woman he's been in a relationship with. And it's not like his relationship with Candace came to an end because they broke up. She *died*! How can I compete with a ghost?

I can't. Not that I'm looking at it as a competition, but knowing he had someone who meant so much to him that he's mourned her loss for this long makes me feel a little inadequate, if I'm honest. Was she the reason he kept pulling away and fighting our chemistry in the beginning? Because he still has feelings for her?

He seemed a little distant after our conversation about her, like he was lost in his thoughts. Not Cold Will level distant, but just off enough that he didn't seem himself. He seemed burdened by something, but I didn't have the strength to ask him. I didn't want to hear him say he missed her. Not while he was still lying naked with me.

I push my thoughts aside, focusing on the problem at hand. I slipped and told my sister about Will. She then told my mom, and now my whole family is insisting they have to meet him. My brothers are especially insistent, given my track record.

I can't really blame them.

I wanted to push it off, but my mom said if I didn't bring him for family dinner this weekend, then she was going to insist he spend Thanksgiving with us.

Will cannot spend Thanksgiving with my family.

My ENTIRE family comes together for Thanksgiving. It's one thing for Will to meet the craziness that is my immediate family, but forcing him to meet the extended family as well?

Yeah, how about I just lead a lamb to slaughter.

Same thing.

So, now Will is going to meet my family. I really hope I've prepared him enough. He's due at my apartment any moment, and my anxiety is already sky high.

A knock pulls me from my mini freak out. I check my hair in the mirror right by the door and then open it, my breath whooshing from my lungs when I see Will.

God, he looks edible.

I bite my lip causing him to grin wide.

"Keep looking at me like that and we won't be seeing your parents tonight."

"Don't tempt me."

"You're one to talk." His eyes scan me from head to toe and then back up. "Fuck, Gina, why do you have to always look so good?"

My heart melts at his compliment, and all my worries from earlier are long forgotten. "Alright, enough with the smooth talking. Let's get this over with."

I grab my purse and off we go.

"They're here!"

My mother's loud voice carries through the door, my finger barely off the doorbell. I thought I'd give Will another minute of peace instead of using my key.

I spent the entire ride reminding Will the names of my siblings, their spouses, and their kids.

The door swings open, my mother standing there with a bright smile on her face while she dries her hands on a towel. She looks great for her age, with only a little salt and pepper in her long black hair currently up in a ponytail. She's wearing a nice blue dress which complements her wide hips.

Birthing hips she calls them.

Lord, help me survive tonight.

She grabs Will and wraps him in one of her signature hugs. "You must be Will. Gina told us you were handsome, but oh my, you are a looker."

"Mami!" I scold.

"What, Cochita? It's not a lie."

Facepalm.

Will just stands there laughing quietly next to me, his eyes alight with joy at my discomfort. He's actually enjoying my torment.

Bastard.

My mom ushers him into the family room, and I hear my titis greet him and also comment on his looks. Oh, Jesus Mary Joseph. She invited her friends?!

I forgot this is how my family gets when I bring a guy home. I must've blocked it out. After all, Collin was the last guy I brought home, and that was over six years ago.

I round the corner and see about five of my beloved "aunts" who I definitely did not expect to see at family dinner, since it's usually just reserved for immediate family.

My nephews and nieces run around playing with their toys and chasing each other, while the baby screams in my sister's arms.

My brothers and brother-in-law are watching ESPN, but their eyes go wide and their jaws drop when they see Will.

I think my brothers thought I was joking when I said I was dating a Wolves player.

My baby brother speaks up first. "Holy shit. She was serious!"

My mom slaps Andres on the arm with the towel still in her hand. "Watch your language in my house, mijo."

Properly chastised, my brother responds, "Yes, Mami."

My mom has taken over the introductions and sweeps Will across the room, introducing him to everyone present. He takes it all in stride—accepting the excited hugs from all the women and the reserved handshakes from the men.

Okay, this isn't so bad.

"So, what're your intentions with my sister?"

Spoke too soon.

"Luis!"

"What?" My oldest brother shrugs. "You have terrible taste in men, so it's only appropriate we properly vet this one."

I'm about to respond when Will beats me to it.

"I'm dating your sister and plan to for as long as she'll have me."

My mom interrupts us before the boys can further question Will. She's carrying a large photo album in her hand.

Oh no. Not my quinceañera album.

"Mami, I'm sure Will doesn't want to see that."

She brushes me off. "I'm sure he does. You were beautiful." She turns to Will. "The two most important days in a woman's life are her quinceañera and her wedding. Our Gina looked absolutely beautiful on her quinceañera."

"She looks beautiful every day."

Will's response causes every woman in the room to let out a sigh while their ovaries internally explode. My brothers simply roll their eyes.

"Is my Cochita here? Is that what all this fuss is about?"

My dad, Ricardo, comes around the corner from outside. He smells like charcoal so I'm guessing he's grilling for dinner tonight.

"Hi, Papi."

"Baby girl." My dad squeezes me in a tight hug. He repositions me to his side and then looks closely at Will.

"So, you're the man my daughter is seeing."

"Yes, sir."

My dad turns to me, his eyes dancing with mirth. "He called me 'sir.' Did you hear that?"

"I did," I say, attempting to conceal the humor in my voice.

My dad turns to my brothers. "How come you rascals can't call me sir?"

My brother Diego responds, "Because you're our dad and it

might give you a big head." He smiles, letting my dad know he's teasing.

My dad just shakes his head and lets out a tut before he turns to Will. "Come outside and help me with the BBQ before Ava starts showing you all of Gina's baby pictures."

I lean into my dad and whisper, "Thank you."

He nods and then exits with Will to the backyard. I'm sure the burgers won't be the only thing getting grilled out there, but at least it won't happen in front of an audience.

My mom rushes over to me. "He's so handsome, Gina."

"I know, Mom."

"Does he treat you well?"

I think about the past year when things were tense and awful between Will and me, but then I think over the last month. Something has definitely changed for Will. He's been in this one hundred percent since our first date and has treated me like a queen. It's been a nice change from the usual guys I date.

"He does. Very well."

She smiles softly at me, her eyes crinkling in the corners. My brothers open their mouths to barrage me with questions, but she silences them with a look.

"That's enough out of you. Will seems like a good man, and we're going to give him a shot, so don't scare him away or I'll let your sister make your lives miserable."

They have the decency to look chagrined. I smile at my mom, thankful for her.

It's amazing how every time we all get together it's like we're still little kids, but I guess that's the nature of siblings.

I look around the room at all the people looking out for me and feel peace settle deep in my bones. I spent most of my childhood trying to be seen and have a place in this family, but I had one all along. No one has ever seen me more clearly than my parents. Sometimes I wonder why I felt so lost growing up, so out of place. When I look at the people gathered here to meet my man, I feel nothing but loved and cared for. I feel seen and protected in a way I never did as a child.

Maybe it's because Will and I talked about exes so recently, or it's just my reflective mood, but I realize not feeling seen at home was often what pushed me to date the guys I did—assholes who still didn't really see me. I glance out the window at Will and my dad by the grill and can't help but think Will might be the first man who's ever truly seen me for me.

Moving closer to my family has only enhanced my desire to work toward building a family of my own, and the more time I spend with Will, the more I start to hope maybe Paige was right and the man for me really *was* in front of me this whole time.

TWENTY-THREE

Will

I follow Gina's dad outside, grateful for the small reprieve. Gina's mom is great, but I could tell her brothers were going to go for the intimidation factor if I stuck around.

I'm waiting for her dad to go that route too.

He doesn't disappoint.

The second he gets to the grill, he turns to me. "What are your intentions with Gina?"

"I want to date her, sir."

"Is that all?"

"It's still new, but I'm in this for as long as Gina will have me."

He stares at me for a moment before nodding. "So, where are you from, Will?"

"Texas, sir."

"Your folks still live there?"

"It's just my mom, but yeah, she still lives there. She moved to Austin recently."

He eyes me closely. "And your dad?"

"He's been out of the picture since I was five. Decided being a dad didn't fit his life."

Ricardo scoffs. "I'm sorry to hear that, son. Your mom must've done a good job if my Gina likes you."

I grip the back of my neck. "According to her and your sons, she's not so good at picking guys."

"She told you that?"

I nod.

He shakes his head. "It's taken a long time for Gina to see her worth. Even when she was a little girl, she wasn't confident about her importance in our family. She allowed that insecurity to guide her in her relationships and chose men who weren't quite worthy. Men who didn't see her value. That's their fault, not hers."

"I agree."

He turns toward me. "Do you see her value?"

I look him dead in the eye. "Yes."

I do. More now than ever.

He refocuses on the grill, setting the burgers every couple of inches apart. I feel the need to elaborate on my answer, to prove I'm worthy of her, even though I'm not entirely convinced I actually deserve her.

"Gina makes me feel something I've never felt before." I pause, debating how much to share with this man I just met. I decide to lay all my cards out there. "I was engaged once."

He pauses his work on the grill but remains still, not looking at me.

"She died in a drunk driving accident."

He turns to me now, sadness coating his features. "I'm so sorry, son."

I nod in recognition of his words.

"I'm telling you this because even though I was engaged and thought I was in love, what I feel for Gina is different. Stronger."

He looks at me closely. "Do you love Gina, Will?"

I'm startled by his question, although I suppose I

shouldn't be given what I've just implied. But I was fooled by love once before, and the idea of being in love again, of giving someone that kind of power over me, is not something I'm ready for.

"I don't know yet. We've only been together a little over a month."

He closes the grill and faces me full-on. "Did Gina tell you how Ava and I met?"

I shake my head.

"We met at the movies. I was there with my buddies, and she was there on a date. The moment I saw her, I knew. I knew she was the woman I would marry. I even tried to interrupt her date by talking to her when her fella went to the bathroom." He laughs and looks down at the ground, shaking his head, then looks back up at me. "She wouldn't give me the time of day. Her date said her name to ask if everything was okay, and I used that to my advantage. I asked around to see if anyone knew her and found out she actually lived in the neighborhood behind mine. We went to rival schools, because of how the zoning worked in our area. I put in a transfer to go to her high school just so I could see her. She was furious when she found out, but eventually went out with me. We've now been married for thirty-eight years."

He looks toward the house, love clear as day all over his face, even all these years later.

"I'm telling you this story because when a man loves a woman, when she's the only woman who will ever complete him, he does *anything* it takes to win her love. He fights for her until the end of time." He points to the house. "I have fought for Ava every day of our marriage. That's what makes a marriage last—when you continue to fight for one another, when you choose to never let your love fade. Love is like a small flame that must always be cared for so it doesn't go out."

He looks me over closely, a small grin on his face. "You'll know when you figure it out."

It almost seems like he thinks I love Gina already, which is crazy. We just got together. Yes, I have intense feelings for her, but that doesn't automatically mean love. I thought I loved Candace, but she proved me wrong in the end.

He turns the conversation to lighter topics while I help him man the grill. And by help him, I mean I basically just stand there and talk to him while he does all the work. I offer to take over a couple of times to give him a break since he's making a feast, but he declines. When Ava comes out to gather the burgers that are already done, I start to understand why.

"How's my Grillmaster doing out here?"

He smiles and blushes. I fight a laugh at how cute Gina's parents are together. I've never witnessed a parental couple act this way. It was never like this between my parents, even before my dad took off.

When we go inside, the table is set with a separate kids' table next to it. There is so much food, I can't imagine we'll even make a dent. When I take a seat, Gina explains all the different options.

"We have the typical American BBQ food—burgers, hot dogs, potato salad—and then we have the Puerto Rican food like arroz con gandules, which is rice and chickpeas, and..." She hesitates, causing me to look at her.

"What?" I ask.

Her eyes shoot to her mom.

"You made pasteles? Mami! When did you even have time to do that?"

Ava looks at Gina with a wide smile on her face. "Of course I made pasteles! This is a big occasion. You haven't brought a man home in years. We wanted to make a good impression and my pasteles are famous."

Gina drops her face into her palm. "Mami, that was totally unnecessary."

"No, it wasn't." Ava scoops up something that looks similar to a tamale but appears to be wrapped in a banana leaf and places it on my plate. "Try it. I'm famous for my pasteles, but it's really a group effort." With that, she turns and heads back into the kitchen.

I turn to Gina for an explanation about what just happened.

"Pasteles take forever to prep and require a lot of people to help. We typically only make them for holidays or special occasions."

She turns to Marisol. "Did you know she was doing this?"

Marisol shrugs and replies, "You know there's no stopping Mom when she gets an idea in her head. The kitchen was filled with women when I came by the other day, so I just turned around and left."

"I can't believe she went to all this trouble."

I take a bite, and barely refrain from groaning with how delicious it tastes. "Damn, that's good."

Within minutes, I've decimated the entire thing, and Ava, who has returned to the table, happily piles two more on my plate.

I lean over to whisper in Gina's ear. "Your mom makes these every holiday?"

She nods.

"We're officially spending all our holidays with your family then, because this is the best thing I've ever eaten."

Her whole face brightens with her smile.

"And what is this drink?" I ask as I take a sip of the concoction that was placed in front of me at some point during the meal.

"Coquito. It's a mixture of coconut milk, rum, and lime juice. Good, right?"

"Mmmhmm," I mumble around a mouthful.

I'm definitely going to need to double my time at the gym tomorrow, but fuck, it's so worth it.

After dinner, we all move back into the family room. Andres walks over to the radio and starts fiddling with it.

"Enough of this old folk's music. Let's turn it up with something a little more upbeat." The music shifts and I quickly recognize the Daddy Yankee song now filling the room. Gina's older brothers grab their wives' hands and start dancing, their kids watching on the sides with big grins on their faces before they start chasing each other around the house. When Marisol's husband scoops her up to join the other couples, I grab Gina's hand and we dance and laugh with the rest of her family.

I catch sight of her dad and mom holding each other with smiles on their faces as they take in the scene before them.

Her dad's eyes meet mine, a knowing look on his face. When I look down at Gina, I wonder if I might actually understand what he was talking about outside after all.

I'm still not convinced what I'm feeling is love, but I know I'd do anything for her.

TWENTY-FOUR

Gina

When Will's sister, Becka, got wind he'd met my family a week ago, she insisted she had to meet me. Since we decided to meet her at the dog park, Will wanted me to join him at his place and then we'd go together from there. I knock on the door and hear Rex's familiar barking. I've met him once and he was the biggest love bug.

Will opens the door, and my jaw drops. A towel hangs low on his waist, water dripping down his chest and six pack. He holds another towel to his hair, attempting to dry the short strands.

Oh.

Yum.

I bite my lip. "Are you sure we have to go to the park? Because, right now, all I can think about is the fact you're naked underneath that towel and it's been too long since I rode you."

He drops the towel he was using to dry his hair and grabs me around the waist, pulling me flush against his tight, chiseled body.

He lets out a deep growl when he notices I'm still feasting

my eyes on his hotness before slamming his mouth down on mine.

God, this man can kiss.

I've never found kissing to be all that sexy, but Will kisses me like he needs my lips to breathe. I moan into his mouth, our tongues now gliding against each other. Will pulls me inside the house and then slams the door shut.

My back hits the closed door, and my hands find the edge of the towel still wrapped around his hips. With one quick tug it falls to the floor, baring him to me.

My fingers wrap quickly around his cock, and I begin stroking his already impossibly hard length, relishing in the soft velvet feel of his thick erection.

Will groans and drops his head to my neck. "Fuck, that feels good."

"Yeah?"

He nods, his head still nestling in my neck, his lips grazing the sensitive spot behind my ear.

Without any warning, I drop to my knees and take him into my mouth. When I glance up, sliding my lips up and down his length, his eyes are molten.

His hand presses on the door at my back in order to hold himself up.

I use my other hand to pump him where my mouth can't reach.

Will is hung.

Like...wow-level hung.

I pump furiously while my lips suck and my tongue licks the underside of his dick.

He groans above me, causing me to glance up to see his reaction to my ministrations.

The look he shoots me is full of fierce heat. When I pull my lips off, he grips the back of my head and slams my head back down on his cock.

My pussy floods with wetness at the roughness of his touch, my clit aching with need for him. I love it when he's like this, demanding and possessive. He controls the pacing and speed and it's so hot, my whole body pulses with an achy longing.

"Fuck, I'm gonna come," he says, his voice hoarse.

He loosens his hold on me, but I keep the pace he held before.

"Gina. If you don't stop, I'm gonna come in your mouth."

I moan around him and take him as far as I can. With a shout, he grips the back of my hair and shoots his hot load down my throat.

"Fuck." He shudders and then gently pulls out of my mouth.

I wipe a remnant of his cum off my lips and then stand up, my legs shaky.

He looks at me reverently, his hand sliding into my hair and holding me close to him. "You're a fucking goddess, you know that?"

"I do believe you've mentioned that before."

He lets out a chuckle, but stops me when I go to move away.

"Where do you think you're going?"

"I was going to go sit in the living room and wait for you to get dressed."

"Nope. It's your turn."

An equal opportunist.

Hell, yes.

It's a clear Southern California day, but the wind has picked up and there's a chill. It's cold enough that I'm wearing a light jacket over my sweater. My jeans and ankle boots complete the ensemble. Will is wearing a long-sleeved shirt that hugs his biceps and hints at his trim waist. His jeans show off his shapely ass, and I'm tempted to grab it.

Damn, he is yummy looking.

"Rex! Come here, boy," a female voice calls from behind us.

Will and I both turn around to see Rex bounding to a young woman who I'm guessing must be Will's sister. Becka is gorgeous. She's model tall with coffee-brown hair, and green eyes that match Will's. She's got a trim figure, but great breasts. I'm actually a little jealous since I'm more on the curvy side, although Will certainly doesn't seem to mind my curves.

Becka has an effortless beauty about her. She walks closer, a kind smile on her face.

"Hey, you must be Gina." Without waiting, she embraces me in a tight hug. "It's so good to meet you." She pulls away and looks at her brother affectionately. "Will's been talking about you for ages."

I turn my head to him and ask, "Is that right?"

"Oh yeah." She leans towards me conspiratorially and adds, "I even guessed you were the girl that had him all in a tizzy over a year ago."

Shock coats my face. "What?"

"Yeah, Will here was pretty pissy about a year or so ago, and I found out it was about a woman, but it was like pulling teeth to get any more information out of him. It wasn't until recently when I put two and two together and he caved and told me you were *her.*"

Will talked about me even back then?

I was not expecting that.

Especially since that was the era of Cold Will. And now that I know about Candace, I can't help but wonder if his behavior was out of guilt for having feelings for another woman when he was still mourning the woman he loved. I glance at

Will to see him staring at Becka with a bright smile on his face—no sign of the distant man he was after he told me about Candace.

Suddenly, Rex barks and bounds toward another dog in excitement, but the poor owner of the other dog looks terrified seeing this big pit bull come racing toward her.

"Shit. I'll be right back," Will says as he goes to chase Rex and calm the terrified woman.

Becka turns back to me. "So, Gina. What are your intentions with my brother?"

"What do you mean?"

"I mean, are you two just messing around, or is this serious?"

"I'm pretty sure it's serious if we're meeting each other's families."

Becka looks over toward Will before turning back to me. "Good. I'm glad he finally let someone in."

"What do you mean?"

She watches her brother as she talks. "Will was really messed up after Candace died. I didn't think he'd ever get over it." She stops and looks closely at me, while my heart drops at her words. "I'm grateful you're in his life. Maybe now he can put all those ghosts behind him."

Rex comes bounding back toward us, grabbing Becka's attention.

Me on the other hand? I'm still stuck on her last statement and the puzzle pieces of Will's past I've collected over the last month. I look over at Will walking back to us. Has he really put Candace behind him?

Or am I just a temporary fix?

Maybe I should've seen Cold Will as the warning of the pain that would come if I let Hot Will into my life.

TWENTY-FIVE

Will

It's surreal having Gina around my sister. Candace only interacted with Becks a couple of times, and they never got along.

That might actually be an understatement.

Becks hated Candace the minute she met her.

Gina, on the other hand, has completely won my sister over. She's even said as much multiple times today. Relief fills me knowing my sister is supportive this time around.

I didn't listen to Becks last time, and it bit me in the ass. Whether I like it or not, my sister can read people better than I can, and I've learned to trust her judgment. It might've saved me a lot of heartache and years of anger and guilt if I had learned that sooner. Knowing she likes Gina lifts a huge weight off of my shoulders.

While Becks clearly loves Gina, I can't get a clear read on where Gina stands. I think she likes Becks because she's been laughing and smiling with her. They've found they have a lot in common and even a mutual friend—someone Gina went to high school with who now works with Becka—but every time Gina looks at me, her eyes dim a little.

It's almost like she's trying to guard herself.

From what, I'm not sure. I thought we were past all that, but maybe I was wrong. I want to ask her about it, but Becks invites herself over for dinner and then Gina leaves as soon as she's done eating, so I never get a chance.

I sit back at the table, sliding my hand through my hair and trying to figure out if I should call Gina tonight to ask her about it. Unease twists in my gut.

"You okay?"

I look at my sister. "Yeah, why?"

"You seem distracted."

"Gina seemed distant with me today, and I wanted to ask her about it, but *someone* had to invite herself to dinner."

She shrugs. "I wanted to keep hanging out. This is the first woman you've dated I actually liked."

"She's only the second woman I've dated."

"Exactly." She throws me a look, but then gets serious. "Gina is really great, Will. I'm so glad you are finally letting someone in. I was worried about you."

"I know you were."

"I even told Gina how grateful I was to her. I thought you'd be hanging on to the ghost of Candace forever."

I still at her words. "When did you tell her that?"

"At the park. Why?"

I think back to when her demeanor changed. Was it what Becka had said that made her attitude shift? The anger that simmers deep in my gut starts boiling to the surface at the thought that once again Candace is getting in the way of me finally being happy.

"Will?"

I shake my thoughts away and try to settle the nerves in my gut and tension in my shoulders. I need to talk to Gina before I start jumping to conclusions.

"No reason. So, how're things with you?"

"Ugh, can we not, please?"

"What? You can hassle me about my life, but I can't hassle you about yours?"

"Yep, pretty much."

I laugh. "Bullshit."

She shrugs and takes another drink of her wine. Her third glass of wine.

"You're staying here tonight."

"That didn't sound like a question."

"It wasn't. If you think I'm going to let you drive home when you've been drinking, you clearly don't know who you're dealing with."

She blanches a little, realizing how close to home that issue is for me.

"Okay. I'll stay, but I'm stealing Rex. I need a cuddle buddy."

Rex perks his head up.

"I swear you're trying to steal my dog from me."

She rubs her hands together like she's the villain in some classic movie. "You're on to my evil plan. Mwahaha."

I laugh. "You're such a weirdo."

"Who do you think I learned it from?"

I roll my eyes. Little sisters.

TWENTY-SIX

Gina

When Will called me asking if I wanted to come over for a movie night at his place, I didn't even hesitate. I missed him, and it'd only been a day.

I pull up to his house, my stomach clenching with nerves and excitement. Becka's comments from yesterday are still lingering in my mind, no matter how many times I've tried to banish them from my thoughts. Will opens the door, a subdued smile on his face, his eyes watching me closely with the slightest hint of concern.

"Hey," he says.

"Hey," I reply softly.

He reaches out and pulls me into his arms, holding me tight. My head rests on his chest, the steady thumping of his heart soothing my nerves. I feel him press his lips to the top of my head and squeeze me tighter to him.

"Is everything okay?"

I pull back just enough to look up at him. "Yeah, why?"

He shrugs. "Yesterday ended weird. It felt like you were pulling away."

"I was just in a weird headspace. We're okay."

"Are you sure? Did Becka say something to upset you?"

His question seems pointed, like he already knows the answer. I note his expression, concern mixed with determination clear on his face.

I could tell him the truth. That she mentioned Candace and it brought up a bunch of internal shit for me. But that would just make me look insecure, and maybe even needy. Two things I don't want to be, especially not now, with Will's arms wrapped around me and his face showing nothing but concern for me. I was probably just being silly. Of course it took Will a long time to get over Candace. She was his fiancée. Anyone would be devastated after such a loss, but it doesn't mean I'm just a replacement or a rebound.

Despite my determination to believe those thoughts, unease still brews deep in my gut.

I look into his eyes, my voice coming out stronger than I expected. "Everything's fine. I promise."

He watches me carefully for another minute or two before he offers a subtle nod and drops a quick kiss on my lips. He slides his hand down my arm and laces his fingers with mine before pulling me gently toward the living room, where I see a movie already queued up on the TV and a bowl of popcorn and two beers sitting on the coffee table.

"Sorry, I didn't have any Milk Duds to throw into the popcorn."

I smile up at him. "I suppose I can forgive you."

He laughs and tugs me close to him as we sit on the couch. We snuggle and watch the movie, and my fears continue to ease. They disappear completely when he starts kissing me. Our mouths mold together like they were made for each other, and my body craves his in a way it never has with another man. Nothing exists but us when we're together like this. No ghosts to interfere in this moment of intimacy as I give myself to him.

It's the middle of the night when we're in bed together, our bodies wrapped around each other, naked and spent from our earlier lovemaking when my fears return with a vengeance. I'm woken up by Will mumbling behind me. At first, I can't tell what he's saying, but the torment in his tone is unmistakable.

I roll over, prepared to wake him up gently from what is obviously a nightmare when I finally hear him clearly. My heart lodges in my throat at the tear sliding down his cheek, his eyes still closed in slumber, and the name he just uttered ringing in my ears.

Candace.

I look in the mirror, admiring my appearance. Will and I are going on our first official double date with Jack and Paige tonight. We both agreed the one two years ago didn't count.

I'm wearing my favorite little black dress, with its sweetheart neckline that makes my breasts look like plush pillows. The dress hugs my hourglass figure like it was made for my body. It has a longer hemline, cutting off midcalf, but has a long slit up the side that makes it exceptionally sexy.

I slide my hand down my hair, hoping to tame any flyaways, and then swipe on my deep red lipstick. My smoky eye makeup enhances the honey color of my brown eyes. I feel like a pinup, and excitement pulses through my body at the idea of what Will's reaction will be.

I never told him what I heard the last time I stayed at his house. After tossing and turning, my mind still reeling from hearing him speak Candace's name with such heartbreak in his voice, I finally fell back into a fitful sleep. I woke up to Will's mouth between my legs and pleasure shooting through my body, his nightmare a distant memory. It wasn't until I was getting dressed while Will made us breakfast that I remembered the night before. I debated with myself whether or not to bring it up but eventually decided against it. Honestly, I wasn't sure I could handle the truth. I just wanted things to be good with us, and I wasn't quite ready to burst the bubble.

I'm still not.

The doorbell rings, and when I open it, Will's reaction does not disappoint. He stands before me in a dark navy suit, his black hair combed and styled, his green eyes heated with lust as his gaze slides over me.

My body flushes with desire, but there's no time for sex right now. Not that that's stopped us lately.

We've been having a lot of sex.

Mind-blowing, life-altering, multiple-orgasm-inducing sex.

My body hums just thinking about it.

"Baby,"—he swipes his hand over his mouth and then down his neck, clearly trying to compose himself—"you look fucking sexy. I can't believe I'm the lucky bastard that gets to have you."

He steps closer, his arm wrapping around my waist and pulling me to him. His mouth drops to my hair, his hot breath sending shivers down my spine.

"But you look even sexier completely naked, no makeup, and hair a mess from my hands being in it."

I look up to him, our eyes giving away our mutual desire.

"Fuck, if we don't get out of here, I'm going to take you right here. And I don't want to mess up your lipstick. You look gorgeous."

I smile. "Thank you. Let me just grab my clutch."

"So, the wedding planner tells me it'll cost ten grand."

"Ten grand for lights?" I ask.

"Yes!" Paige lets out a frustrated sigh. "That's ridiculous. I don't want to spend a fortune on what is essentially just a big party. At the end of the day, it's not the wedding that matters, it's the marriage. I read an article that said the more you spend on a wedding, the higher your odds of a divorce."

I nod. "I saw that article too."

"I told her we could just elope. Invite our families and closest friends and call it a day." Jack grabs Paige's hand, a look of love passing between them. "All that matters to me is I get to call you my wife."

Will laughs into his drink. "You've already started calling her your wife."

Paige and I both look at Will in surprise.

Paige then turns to Jack. "You have?"

He nods, a blush forming on his cheeks. "Yeah. I mean, you basically are already anyway. At this point it's just a formality."

I'm pretty sure if Paige wasn't completely in love with him already, this moment would've sealed the deal. Her face glows with pure, unadulterated love for him.

God, these two make my heart so happy, especially after everything they've been through.

I look at Will, wondering if we might make it like Paige and Jack have.

Okay, maybe I'm getting a little ahead of myself. Just because I'm ready for marriage and a family doesn't mean Will is. Surprisingly, it's not something we've talked about in any of our conversations.

But we've been together for two months now, and it's been heaven. I've never felt like this with anyone before. Not even with Collin, and I was with him for almost two years.

It's crazy, but sometimes you just know when someone is right for you.

Will looks over at me and grabs my hand, bringing it to his

mouth and placing a gentle kiss. My heart melts, and I'm pretty sure if I was a cartoon, now is when hearts would be shooting out of my eyes.

"I need to use the ladies' room. Gina?"

"What is it with girls always having to go to the bathroom together?" Jack asks.

"Dude, don't even ask. It's a thing. Just accept it. My sisters told me I wouldn't understand 'cause I was a guy, so why bother even trying," Will responds.

I smile at Will and nod. "Your sisters were right." I lean over to place a kiss on his cheek, forgetting about my lipstick and leaving a light smudge on his face. "We'll be right back."

When Paige and I get to the bathroom, I go straight to the mirror to touch up my lipstick while Paige goes inside one of the stalls.

"So, is everything else going well wedding-wise, besides the lights?" I ask.

"Yeah, my brothers are going to come to the wedding, which I'm really excited about. It's been forever since I've seen them. It sucks they live so far away, but there's nothing like a wedding to bring a family together. Speaking of weddings, what's going on with you and Will?"

I stop what I'm doing and turn to Paige as she opens the stall door. "How in the hell do you go from weddings to Will and me?"

"Well, you two seemed really cozy out there, and the only times you've been free to hang out have been when the guys are away, otherwise you're *busy*," she says with a knowing grin.

I turn back to the mirror, double-checking my hair. "Things are really good."

"Yeah?"

I stop and turn to Paige, my lip caught between my teeth as I debate revealing what I've been holding back.

"I think I'm in love with him," I whisper.

"What?" Her smile is wide.

"It's crazy, right?" I look back in the mirror, attempting to wrap my head around this. "We've only been together for two months. That's way too soon, right?"

"To be in love?"

I nod.

"Not at all. I knew I loved Jack after a month. Actually, I loved him from the moment we first reconnected, but I was in denial."

"Yeah, but you two had history."

"So do you and Will," she aptly points out. "You two have been dancing around each other for two years. Now you're finally together, it doesn't surprise me at all you'd fall in love with him after two months."

"I guess."

"This is a good thing, Gina."

I certainly hope so, because deep down I'm terrified I'm not enough for Will. That maybe I'm just a replacement for the fiancée he lost.

That while he might be the love of my life, maybe he's already had his.

TWENTY-SEVEN

Will

I took a deep breath and gripped my neck, searching for the strength to do what I needed to do. I walked into the living room where Candace was sitting on the couch watching TV.

"Hey, can we talk?"

She didn't look at me right away, but when she did, I could tell she knew what was coming. Her gaze was cautious as it landed on mine. Maybe she would understand. Maybe she could tell things had changed between us too. That even though there had been love and affection between us, something still felt like it was missing.

She nodded and then cleared her throat. "I think that'd be a good idea actually."

She looked down at her hands, fidgeting with her fingers before I saw her heave a deep breath and look up at me with tears in her eyes. I was expecting her to cry, but not before I actually got the words out.

"I think we should break up."

"I'm pregnant."

Her words were jumbled with mine, so it took me a minute to realize what she just said.

"Wait, you're what?"

She took a deep breath and then looked me in the eye. "I'm pregnant."

"But we've always used condoms," I said, dumbfounded on how this could've happened when I've worked so hard to prevent this very thing.

"Condoms aren't one hundred percent reliable."

"But you're also on birth control. Shouldn't that count as double protection?"

She hesitated for the briefest of moments before responding. "I stopped taking them awhile back because I was planning to switch to something different."

I sat down heavily on the couch next to her, my body sagging with the weight of what this meant. I couldn't break up with her now. I swore to myself if I ever had a kid, I would never leave him. I would never be a part-time dad. I wouldn't be MY dad. I refused.

Which meant, I had no other choice here. Not really.

I scrubbed my hands up and down my face, trying to breathe while my heart dropped into my stomach at the fact I was about to do the exact opposite of what I had planned only five minutes ago.

How quickly things change.

I turned to Candace and took in her calm, quiet demeanor, which was so completely opposite to mine. While my inner voice screamed at me, I said the words I hadn't expected to say to Candace.

"I think we should get married."

When the girls round the corner and disappear into the bathroom, Jack turns to me, a huge grin on his face.

"Seems like you and Gina are doing well."

I nod and take a sip of my drink. "Yeah. We are. She's one hell of a woman."

"I'm happy for you, man."

"Thanks."

"Seriously, though,"—his face sobers—"I didn't know if I'd ever get to see you happy again. I saw what it did to you to lose Candace. I know you were really struggling."

Except he doesn't. He doesn't know at all how I struggled or why I felt so guilty.

Why I *still* feel guilty.

My body feels heavy with the weight of all the emotions Candace's memory brings out in me. Emotions that have been exposed like raw nerve endings since my nightmares started back up. Thankfully, none have happened when Gina's slept over. I don't even know how I'd begin to explain them to her.

I'm not ready to tell her the truth.

I shrug. "Yeah, well, Gina's great."

My response feels lame. Gina is so much more than great. She's everything I've ever dreamed of finding in a woman. She's the whole damn package, and I know I don't deserve her.

That doesn't stop me from wanting her.

Jack takes a sip of his whiskey. "I really am glad to see you moving on. I think Candace would want you to be happy."

No, she wouldn't.

She lived to make me miserable. To control me and manipulate me in ways I was blind to until the end.

That thought sends ice through my body, and I freeze up. I think again about the nightmares I've started having, the dreams of her crying and screaming at me.

She's still making me miserable even in death.

I just shrug, not knowing what to say to him and trying not

to get lost in my own thoughts. He watches my reaction closely and then smirks again and shakes his head.

"You know, I never thought you'd fall in love again."

My head snaps up, my gaze locked on him. "What?"

Shock must cover my face because he laughs at my reaction like he's surprised.

"Don't deny it, man."

I lean forward. "I like Gina. That's it. It's still new."

"Keep lying to yourself buddy."

"I'm not lying."

He pins me with a serious look. "Bullshit. You look at Gina the way I look at Paige. I recognize love when I see it."

I sit back in my chair, stunned into silence, as I replay moments with Gina in my head.

Love?

No. It's not love.

Lust? Fuck, yes.

Like? Definitely.

Love? Not a chance.

I know what I feel for Gina is different than Candace, but I don't believe in love, not after what Candace put me through. I've never been in love, even if I once thought I was. That wasn't love. Gina might be different than Candace but I can't love her. I can't.

"I'm happy with Gina, that's it. Don't go putting labels on it that don't belong there."

He frowns slightly and shakes his head at me. "Whatever you say, man. It's not a death sentence to love someone."

He has no idea how wrong he is.

If history is any indication, it's a death sentence to love me.

I can't let myself go there with Gina.

I won't.

Suddenly, it feels hot and suffocating in here. How did I get myself into this situation? How did I let myself forget all the reasons why I held myself back from Gina originally?

Just then, I glance up and see Gina and Paige talking animatedly, smiles on their beautiful faces as they return to the table.

Paige leans down and kisses Jack soundly on the lips before sitting in her seat. He watches her, love clear as day plastered all over his face.

I definitely don't look at Gina that way.

Do I?

Gina makes her way to our side of the table and sits down gracefully in her seat. Her hand finds mine, and she shoots me a dazzling smile.

My heart stutters in my chest and my breath stalls in my lungs.

Fuck.

How did this happen?

I can't be in love with her.

I can't.

I barely survived Candace dying, and I didn't love her at all, not like I once thought I did.

I look at Gina, watching her sip her water and begin a discussion with Paige. About what I have no clue, because I feel like the room is a vacuum, my ears ringing and everything disappearing except for Gina.

If I only know one thing, it's that I'd never survive losing her.

I'm a zombie the rest of dinner. Gina picks up on it faster than Paige and Jack. I provide minimal responses to the conversation and spend most of the evening staring at my food.

At one point, Gina slides her hand over my thigh, giving it a gentle squeeze. When I look over at her, she gives me a questioning look, but I ignore it and focus again on my food and attempt to follow along with whatever Jack and Paige are saying.

I can't ease her concerns right now. Not when I'm freaking out at my own revelation.

Why did Jack have to say anything?

Couldn't he have left me in ignorance?

By the time dinner finishes, I've nearly shut down completely.

I don't even hold Gina's hand on the way to the car.

"Will?" Her voice is soft and hesitant, but it doesn't break the resolve growing in my gut. "Are you okay? You were awfully quiet at dinner."

"I'm fine," I reply shortly, my tone indicating I'm not in the mood to talk.

Gina doesn't press further. She glances at me several times on the drive back to her place, especially when I make the turn for her apartment instead of the other direction which would take us to my house. She's been staying at my house when I'm in town since I have Rex. I'm sending a clear message by taking her to her apartment.

I walk her to the door, because no matter what I'm feeling internally right now, I'm still the gentleman my mom raised.

"Will? Seriously, is everything okay?" she asks again.

I don't miss the insecurity in her question. She told me once she used to think of me as Cold Will or Hot Will. It was a little funny at the time, but I can tell by her expression and the worry in her eyes she sees what I'm doing.

Cold Will is coming back with a vengeance.

A small part of me realizes I'm making a mistake—an error I might not be able to come back from—but I can no longer stop it. My defenses were trained well by Candace, and they are rising up strong and firm to protect me from getting hurt again.

"It's fine. Just tired. I'll talk to you later." I drop a kiss to her cheek—unable to even kiss her lips for fear it would warm my ice-cold heart and bring me back to her.

I leave her standing outside her door and walk straight to my car.

I never look back.

TWENTY-EIGHT

Gina

Cold Will is back.

I'm angry at myself for letting my guard down, but more than that, I'm terrified about what this means for *us*. Is Will going to pull away again? Is he going to break up with me?

Is this about me? Or is it about Candace?

I guess, more importantly, does the reason even matter?

He drops a kiss to my cheek—not even my lips—and my heart splinters in my chest.

Please don't do this, Will.

Please don't pull away again.

Not now.

Not when I've finally fallen in love with you.

He leaves me standing outside my door, and I watch him walk to his car without ever looking back.

The second I get inside my apartment, the tears fall, and I don't bother stopping them.

It's been over a week since I've seen Will. I tried calling him the day after our double date, but he blew me off. I was convinced he was ghosting me until he finally returned my text saying he had to go out of town suddenly for some Under Armour promo.

I believed him until Paige called asking if I wanted to hang out while our guys were golfing with some of their teammates.

Golfing in LA. When Will claimed he had a promo in New York.

My heart cracked a little further at that.

What's killing me the most is I don't understand what changed. I thought we were doing okay.

But then the vicious voice in my head speaks up. *Was it? Was it really going well? Or were you just a replacement for his dead fiancée? The first and only other relationship he's ever had. How can you compare to the first woman who had his heart? The same woman he would now be married to if she hadn't died?*

He wouldn't have chosen you.

And isn't that the real kicker in the situation? That damn voice is right. Under other circumstances, Will and I would never be together. He'd be happily married to Candace, a woman he rarely opens up about. I can only assume he's so closed off where she's concerned because it hurts too much to talk about her.

How can I compete with a ghost?

Do I even want to?

The answer is no.

I want to be someone's first choice, not the consolation prize.

I drive to Will's house determined to get some kind of resolution. He's been cold and distant for long enough. I can't keep living in this limbo with him. It's too hard. I'd rather know where we stand.

I park my car in front of his house, take a deep breath, and then make my way to the front door. His surprise at seeing me standing on his porch is to be expected.

What wasn't expected is the pain that flashes across his eyes when he invites me in.

I don't know how to take that.

"Gina. What are you doing here?"

"I thought it was time we talked. Can I come in?"

He nods and steps aside, allowing me to enter the house. I look around the room and immediately notice the silence.

"Where's Rex?"

"Becks wanted to take him to the dog park."

I nod my head in understanding. Will watches me carefully and tucks his hands in the pockets of his gray sweats. "So, you wanted to talk?"

His expression is guarded, making me wish with everything I have that I could read his mind right now.

What is he thinking?

Has he missed me like I've missed him? Has he missed me at all?

I clear my throat, hoping to remove the emotion from my practiced speech. "You've been distant for over a week now. I want to know why."

"I told you, I've been busy. I had promos and stuff."

"The Under Armour promo in New York, you mean?"

"Yeah."

I nod my head slowly. "Interesting, because Paige called to see if I wanted to hang out while you were golfing with Jack the day you were supposed to be doing those promos."

His face blanches, and he has the decency to look ashamed.

I watch his hand slide through his hair and then grip the base of his neck, his gaze glued to the floor.

"Why would you lie to me, Will?"

He doesn't answer. Just stands there staring at the floor. I fight the urge to scream at him to get him to show some kind of emotion. Anything!

I step closer, placing my hand on his chest. His eyes slowly slide up my body, heating me as they trace my curves before meeting my eyes.

"I can't stand that you lied, Will,"—my voice cracks but I push on—"I thought we were more than that. You know my history with guys, most of them liars. I didn't think you'd fall in that category."

His eyes look haunted, and anguish flashes through them before he grips the back of my head and devours my mouth with his own.

I let his kiss pull me under before my senses scream at me to force him to talk. I pull away slightly, just barely breaking our connection.

"Will." His name is a plea on my lips. A plea for the truth. A plea for reassurance that we're okay. A plea that he'll finally open himself up to me fully, that he'll give himself to me the way I've given myself to him.

A plea for him to love me. To *choose* me.

His lips crash down on mine again, and his tongue delves into my mouth, owning me with his kiss.

In this moment, I am his, and he is mine.

Whether he'll admit it with words or not.

But I want more than just his body. I want his heart, the way he has mine.

With that thought, I finally break away from his kiss and step back, hoping distance will give us both clearer heads so we can deal with whatever is going on with him.

He stares at me for a minute, his breaths coming out heavy as he recovers from our kiss. With a groan, he turns away from me and grips his hair with both his hands. When he turns back to me, the look of regret on his face causes my stomach to drop.

No.

Please, God, don't let him do this.

"Will?" I ask again softly, my heart clenching in anticipation of the blow I can already see coming.

"I don't know if I can do this anymore."

I bite my lip, barely holding back the tears I can feel stinging my eyes. "Is it because I'm not Candace?" I ask, finally voicing my deepest fear.

He huffs out a laugh. "You're definitely not Candace."

Four words have never hurt as much as those do when they leave his lips. I've suspected for a while that he might still be hung up on her, but hearing him confirm I don't measure up sends pain straight to my already breaking heart.

Without a word, I turn away from him, trying to compose myself, but I feel the pinprick of tears in my eyes and know if I stay any longer, I will completely expose my heartache to him.

Will must sense the change in me. "Gina?"

"Don't bother, okay? I get it. You don't want to do this anymore? Fine. We're done."

A tear slips out and I brush it away furiously. I want to say more to him, but emotion clogs my throat and all I can get out is, "Goodbye, Will."

I walk to my car, while pain slices through me at the realization I never had his heart, and wishing with everything I have that he would give me mine back.

What I hate most is that a part of me wishes he'd come out to fight for me.

But he doesn't.

I drive away, tears blurring my vision to the point where I

have to pull over in order to compose myself. All I can do now is pray that someday I'll finally find someone who thinks I'm enough.

TWENTY-NINE

Will

Our closest friends congratulated us as Candace gushed about how fabulous our wedding was going to be. Her words, not mine. I would've been content just having a courthouse wedding or running off to Vegas. This was the first moment where Candace actually felt like a gold digger, even though I knew she didn't need my money. Her parents were loaded. Completely neglectful and total assholes, but loaded nonetheless.

Things had been...tense between us. I'd been working through my own issues, trying to come to terms with the reality I was going to be a father and I was about to marry a woman I wasn't sure I loved anymore. A woman who changed more every day to the point where I'd started wondering if I ever really knew her at all.

Becka begged me not to do it. Reminded me that couples had kids without getting married all the time—but that's not the life I envisioned for my kid. It probably stemmed from my own upbringing, but I'd always felt very strongly about the fact that I would be married to the mother of my child.

I looked over at Candace and caught her gaze. She smiled at me, seemingly unaffected by this major life change coming our *way, and gently rubbed her stomach. I might've been uneasy about things right now, but I wouldn't let my kid down. I was doing this for him or her, and from here on out my child would always come first. I pasted a smile on my face and turned back to our friends, hoping no one could pick up the uncertainties that plagued me.*

Numbness pumps through my veins as I lift the weight over my head robotically. I've been in the gym for two hours, hoping to wear myself out to the point of exhaustion. It's been three days since I let Gina walk out of my house and my life.

My muscles shake, forcing me to focus on the weight I'm trying to bench press. I hear the door open and feet shuffle nearby, but I ignore it.

Whoever it is can go fuck themselves. I'm in no mood to talk to anyone.

"Will? Fuck, dude, you shouldn't be benching that much without a spotter. Are you fucking insane?"

"I'm fine," I spit out between clenched teeth just as my grip starts slipping. Jack catches it before it drops on me and helps me guide it back onto the rack.

"What's going on with you? You've been MIA for days."

"Didn't feel like talking to anyone."

"Are you okay?"

How can he even fucking ask me that?

I turn a scornful look to him. "Are you fucking kidding me? No, Jack. I'm not okay. You really think I'd be okay after Gina and I broke up? I just want to forget anything exists besides football," I say as I turn back to the weights.

Jack's face falls as my words register. "You and Gina broke up? When?"

I look at him, confused. Surely Paige would've told him. "Three days ago. Paige didn't tell you?"

He grips the back of his neck. "I don't think she knows." He immediately pulls out his phone and starts texting. I can only assume he's texting Paige.

But why wouldn't Gina tell her?

"She hasn't talked to Gina?"

He shakes his head, his eyes still glued to his phone. "She's been reaching out to her the past few days but with minimal response. She figured Gina was just busy with you, but clearly that wasn't the case."

No. Gina definitely wasn't with me.

Her face when I said she wasn't Candace still haunts me. I know she took it wrong, but I was already in a downward spiral at that point and didn't correct her.

I didn't tell her she was so much more than Candace ever was.

That she owned me, and that scared the shit out of me.

It's better this way. At least I didn't get any deeper with her, although I can't help but wonder if it's a little too late. My heart's already involved, and it seems all I've done is watch it walk out the door with Gina.

Jack finally looks up from his phone and stares at me.

I know what I look like. I haven't slept more than a few hours here and there, bags under my eyes, sweat dripping from my body, and my shoulders sagging in defeat.

Jack squats in front of me. "What the hell happened, Will?"

I shrug. "It doesn't matter."

"I think it does."

"It really doesn't. This is for the best."

"What? You punishing your body endlessly in a weak attempt to fix your broken heart?"

I glare at him.

"You forget who you're talking to. I've been in your shoes. I've lost the girl before, remember?"

"I didn't lose Gina."

"Really?" he says doubtfully. "'Cause from where I'm sitting it sure as shit doesn't look like you have her."

"I never had her to begin with!" I shout, my feelings finally overwhelming me. "I never fucking had her. She wasn't supposed to mean anything. And then you had to go ahead and point out I was in love with her. Well, fuck you!" I take a breath, fighting my emotions and trying to hold back the burning in my eyes while I rub my chest hoping to ease the persistent ache.

"She doesn't deserve someone like me."

That's what it all boils down to. I was never good enough for her. Not with my history. Not with what happened with Candace. Gina doesn't need someone like me.

"What does that mean?"

I shrug, losing all energy to continue having this conversation.

Jack just stares at me for another moment before sliding his hand through his hair in frustration.

"Will, when was the last time you saw your therapist?"

"I stopped a while ago. I didn't need to see him anymore. I got my starting position back, and things were good with..." I trail off, remembering my feelings for Gina were the main reason I stopped going to therapy. I thought I'd worked through enough of my issues since things had been going so well with her.

I replay the last time I saw her. The pain in her eyes that she tried so hard to hide from me.

Not for the first time, I wonder if I stopped therapy prematurely.

"When things were good with Gina?" Jack asks, finishing the word I left unsaid.

My heart clenches painfully in my chest.

Fuck, when is this going to stop hurting?

I can't speak, so I just nod.

"I think maybe you should try to schedule an appointment with him."

I stand up, grabbing my water bottle from the floor, and start walking out.

"Will. I'm serious."

My throat is tight from holding back all my emotions, so I just toss a wave back and leave the gym.

The quietness of my house is numbing, or maybe that's all the alcohol. I tip back the last swig of my ninth beer. Or is it my tenth?

Fuck it. Who cares?

I attempt to stand up to grab another beer from the fridge, determined to drown myself in alcohol, but I don't even make it all the way up before my body weight shifts and I find myself face first in the couch.

I drop the beer bottle to the floor and close my eyes, sagging farther into the couch. I feel Rex jump up and curl up by my legs.

At least I'm not totally alone. I move my hand to pat Rex on the head. His tongue sweeps out to lick my arm, and again, I wonder if I rescued him, or if he's rescuing me.

"I fucked it all up, buddy."

Despite all the alcohol coursing through my bloodstream, my thoughts about Gina are still crystal clear, my pain only partially muted. My yearning for her is still sharp, though.

"Why did I do this?"

That question burns through my brain and seeps into my dreams when the alcohol finally puts me to sleep.

When I wake up, it's the first thought I have, followed by the hurt in Gina's eyes the last time I saw her.

Fuck, I miss her so much.

I sit up, my head pounding and the bright light coming through the window blinding me. I pick up my phone and dial. A woman answers on the third ring, which is painful to my hungover ears.

"I need to make an appointment."

THIRTY

Gina

Pounding on my front door pulls my gaze from the television. I furrow my brow, curious who it could be. I'm not expecting anyone.

Hell, I've been avoiding people for days. I even got permission from my boss, Victoria, to work from home, which allowed me to hide my puffy eyes from others and ignore what I'm sure would be a million questions from Paige.

She thinks I've been with Will.

The incessant pain in my chest reminds me I won't be with Will ever again.

Another knock pulls me from my thoughts, and I push myself from the couch, readjusting my shirt and tamping down my crazy hair on my way to the peephole.

"I know you're in there."

Damn. My shoulders sag as I shuffle to the door and unlock it, opening it to see my best friend standing there, concern clear as day on her expressive face.

"Gina, you look terrible."

I choke out a laugh. "Wow, thanks. Kick a girl while she's down, why don't you."

She doesn't smile. "Why didn't you tell me about Will?"

"How'd you find out?"

"Jack."

Figures. I open the door wider and gesture for her to enter. She takes the invitation and walks past me. As soon as I shut the door, I turn to see her standing before me, her arms crossed and her expression a mix of concern and frustration.

"So, why did I have to find out from my fiancé that you and Will broke up?"

"Do you ever get tired of calling him your fiancé?"

A brief smile graces her lips. "No." Her expression gets stern again. "Stop trying to distract me. Seriously, Gina. Why would you go through this alone? Especially after our double date. I mean, you told me you loved him."

A piece of hair falls into my eye, so I brush it aside and move to the couch, not making eye contact with Paige.

"I don't want to talk about it."

"Tough shit. I do. What the hell happened with you two? I thought you guys had finally worked through everything."

"So did I," I whisper, my heart clenching in my chest. A tear slips silently down my already splotchy cheek.

The couch bends from Paige's weight when she sits next to me, her arm going around my shoulders. The affection is all it takes to send me over the edge, a sob ripping from my throat and the dam breaking.

Paige holds me while I cry, rocking us back and forth, offering whispered words of support and encouraging me to get it all out.

Why does this hurt so badly? It never hurt like this when I left Collin, and he cheated on me, which felt like the ultimate betrayal.

I'm not sure how long I cry in Paige's arms, but the shoulder of her shirt is soaked from my tears when they finally slow. She rubs my back while I slowly come down from the emotional release. What is it about crying so hard that just exhausts you? I feel worn out, my limbs heavy, and like I could sleep for days.

I sit up, pulling away from the comfort of Paige's arms, thankful for my friend's love and support. She should be mad at me for not telling her, but she isn't.

She leans over to my coffee table and grabs a tissue for me to wipe my face and blow my nose.

"Thanks," I say.

She nods, watching me attempt to pull myself together. "What happened?"

"I wasn't enough." My throat tightens a little when I speak. "I can't compete with his dead fiancée. Did you know she was his first ever relationship?"

She shakes her head.

I grab another tissue from the box on the coffee table and dab under my eyes. "He really loved her, and I can't compete with that. He doesn't love me like he loved her. I think he might even still love her."

I don't look at her face, instead choosing to fidget with the tissue in my hand, pulling it apart.

How appropriate, since I feel like I'm constantly being pulled apart.

She places her hand on my arm. "Did you tell him you loved him?"

I shake my head.

"Why not?"

"What's the point? He can't love me like I deserve." I turn my body to her, finally making eye contact. "I want to be someone's first choice. Don't I deserve that?"

She nods, her eyes reflecting the sadness I feel coursing through my body.

"I'm not Will's first choice. He's still mourning the loss of his fiancée. Maybe someday he'll be over it, but I can't keep loving him knowing he doesn't feel that way about me."

My shoulders sag in defeat once again. "I wish I didn't love him. Hell, right now I wish I never even met him."

"You don't mean that."

"I really do."

She shakes her head in disbelief, then looks around my apartment, taking in the evidence that I've been pretty useless for the past three days. Dishes are piled in the sink, crumbs cover my coffee table, and tissues are strewn all over the floor from my many bouts of crying.

She brings her gaze back to me, fully taking in how awful I look. I'm sure I also stink, which makes me wince a little knowing she had to smell me while I cried in her arms.

"Okay, here's what we're going to do. Why don't you jump in the shower? I'm going to pick up this place a bit and then we're going to go out and get some food. I'm thinking pizza, ice cream, maybe even some popcorn and Milk Duds. Then we're going to come back here and veg out with an epic girls' night. Sound like a plan?"

It certainly sounds better than wallowing in my pain like I've been doing for the past three days.

"Okay."

"Okay, go hop in the shower. You reek."

"Gee, thanks. Don't hold back when I'm already suffering."

Her eyes soften, and she places her hand on my arm. "You're going to get through this, and I'll be right beside you the whole time." Guilt mars her face. "I know I kept trying to push you and Will together. I really thought you two would be perfect for each other, but I promise I won't do that again. If he can't see how amazing you are, then he doesn't deserve you. And he's had more than enough chances."

I nod my head in agreement, afraid if I try to speak, I might cry again. Without another word, I head to the bathroom, prepared to wash away all my heartache and start the long process of moving on.

My car idles, the warm air wrapping around me and keeping me comfortable despite the cold chill in the late November air outside. I glance out the passenger window, seeing my parents' house lit up. Despite how inviting it looks, I'm terrified of going in there, knowing everyone is here for Thanksgiving. I haven't told my family yet about Will and me, but I know they're going to ask about him.

I take a deep, fortifying breath and close my eyes, attempting to find the courage to tell my parents Will and I broke up.

Tap, tap, tap.

I slam my back against my seat, my hand clutching my chest, which houses my pounding heart.

"Hey, open up." I look over at the passenger door to see Marisol standing there, her cream sweater wrapped tightly around her body. I unlock the doors, still trying to calm myself down from the fright my sister just gave me.

She opens the door and sits down in the passenger seat, quickly shutting the door behind her to keep as much of the warm air in the car as possible.

"You gave me a fucking heart attack," I state.

"Sorry," she shrugs. "But mom wanted to know why you were just sitting out in your car like a weirdo, so I volunteered to see what was up. Are you planning to come in tonight?"

"Of course I am. I've only been out here for, like, five minutes."

She gives me a weird look. "You've been out here for thirty minutes."

I look quickly at the clock. Has it really been that long already?

Shit.

She readjusts in the seat, giving me that sisterly look. You know the one. The one where she knows something is wrong and she's prepared to sit there until she finally pulls it out of me.

"So? What's going on?"

Do I fight this inquisition, or do I give in? I think about the relief that came with finally spilling my guts to Paige and decide to open up to my sister.

"Will and I broke up."

Shock registers on her face, but to her credit she tries to cover it quickly. "I'm so sorry, Gina. You two seemed really happy when we met him. What happened?"

"He had a fiancée three years ago who died."

She rests her palm on her heart. "Oh my God. Poor Will." Her voice quakes with emotion. She's become extremely emotional since having baby Alex. She blames the hormones. I think it's because becoming a mom has made her a big sap.

"Yeah, she was also his first serious relationship."

"God, I can't even imagine how hard that must've been for him. How did she die?"

"A drunk driver."

Marisol just shakes her head, clearly sympathizing with Will's tragedy.

"So, what does this have to do with you?"

I look down at the hem of my sweater, pulling the ends with my fingers to avoid making eye contact. "He's still in love with her, I think."

"You think?"

I nod.

"You don't know? Did he say something that made you think this?"

I shrug. "It was just a bunch of little things and comments he's made…and his sister made." I think back to that last night we were together.

A tear slips down my cheek as I choke out, "He told me I wasn't her."

"Oh, Gina."

I look up to see my sister tearing up. She reaches out and pulls me to her. The hug is awkward over the middle console, but I accept it anyway, relishing the warmth and comfort from my big sister.

She pulls back. "I hate that you're hurting. What can I do?"

I laugh-cry. "Keep our brothers from going after him."

She looks toward the house and then back to me, doubt all over her features. "Yeah, I'm not sure I can follow through on that one."

I lean back against my seat. "How do I tell everyone?"

"Let me handle it. Give me five minutes and then come in. That'll give you some time to compose yourself and fix your mascara, which is running down your face at the moment."

I grab the overhead mirror and look. "Oh, jeez. I look like a freaking raccoon."

"It's fixable. Don't worry. I got you, Cochita."

Turning back to my sister, I offer her another quick hug. "Thanks, Mari. I owe you one."

"No, you don't. Family looks out for each other. That's what we do."

I nod, trying not to tear up again.

She gets out of the car, and I spend the next five minutes putting my emotions on lockdown. I fix my makeup and pinch my cheeks, hoping it'll distract from my red eyes.

Five minutes after Marisol entered the house, I open the

door and walk through my parents' living room to see my parents, aunts, and uncles congregating between the dining room and kitchen, while my cousins, my brothers, their spouses, and all their kids hang around the living room watching TV. True to her word, Marisol's handled the situation. No one asks about Will or why I've so obviously been crying. The only hint they give that they know what happened is that my brothers each give me a hug before we sit down to eat.

They also don't tease me about anything, which is a dead giveaway that Marisol told them the whole story and warned them to be on their best behavior.

I've never been so thankful for my family as I am tonight, watching them interact at the dinner table, telling jokes or talking about anything but football, which is something they would normally be discussing endlessly.

When I leave, I give my sister an extra-long hug and a thank you, and then make my way home.

Walking into my empty apartment, I look around while I place my purse and keys on the table beside the door. Loneliness sweeps through me and tears prick my eyes. I bite my lip, attempting to fight back the tears before they breach my lids and slide down my cheeks, but to no avail. The second the first one slips out, I let out a choked sob and slide down the door, holding my knees close to my body in an attempt to comfort myself.

Everywhere I look, I see signs of Will. The couch where he bent me over and fucked me until I saw stars before we ended up cuddling and watching re-runs of *The Office*. The kitchen where we cooked a meal together and made a huge mess, laughing the whole time. My room just down the hall where I would wake up wrapped in his arms feeling safer than I ever have before.

I don't want to be here right now. Not while I still feel so raw. As my tears start to slow, I pull out my phone from my pocket and look up flights to Puerto Rico.

Needing some distance from LA and all the memories it holds of a man I let myself fall desperately and deeply in love with, I decide it's time I went to visit my abuela for a while.

THIRTY-ONE

Will

I stared at my friend and teammate, Luke Carter, refusing to believe the words that just came out of his mouth. This wasn't happening. This couldn't be happening. I gripped my hair and shook my head, wanting the words hanging heavy in the air to disappear.

"She must've misunderstood," I told him.

He shook his head at me sadly. "I was worried you might think that. I had her send me the screenshots. Anna doesn't have a reason to lie about this. I'm sorry, man. I wish it weren't true, but here's the proof, if that's what you need."

He dug his phone out of his pocket and opened up a stream of texts from his current girlfriend. He scrolled up and showed me the screenshots of my fiancée—and the supposed mother of my goddamn child—bragging about how easy it was to trap me when she suspected I was planning to break up with her. I read the messages that were apparently sent to a group of women, one of whom was seeking advice because she thought her guy was going to dump her.

My heart stopped in my chest when I saw the line Luke specifically told me about. "You should've seen Will's face when

I told him I was pregnant. I had him hook, line, and sinker then. I knew he'd never be able to say no to his baby. And I figure once we're married in a few weeks, I'll just tell him I lost it and he'll never be the wiser."

My heart broke as I realized it was all a lie.

She was never pregnant.

She lied to me, deceiving me over something I was actually starting to get excited about. For what? She didn't need my money or my fame. Why would she do this to me?

Then it hit me, harder than being tackled to the ground.

Control.

She's been manipulating me and controlling me this whole fucking time.

None of what I thought we had was real.

With that thought came a burning rage I'd never felt before. I shoved the phone against Luke's chest and stomped toward the door, determined to end this relationship for good.

The soft leather of the couch dips from my weight. The moment I entered the small room, the hint of vanilla that hit my nose made my heart ache with memories of Gina. She always used to smell like vanilla, something she claimed was because of the scented lotion she used.

"So, Will, what's been going on?"

I shift my jaw back and forth, rubbing the unfamiliar stubble—from too many days not shaving—with my calloused hand.

"I think I quit therapy prematurely."

I expect a reaction, but Dr. Stein has a stone-cold poker face.

"Why do you think that?"

Taking a deep breath in an attempt to strengthen my resolve, I say quietly, "Because I fucked up."

His eyes squint minutely. "Care to elaborate?"

I look him dead in the eye. "I fell in love."

"Okay."

I drop my head in my hands, and then run my fingers through my hair as I sit back up. I'm not the most eloquent guy on a good day, but add the emotional stress I've been dealing with and it makes finding the words harder.

"I didn't mean to, but I fell in love with her."

"Is it safe to presume the woman to whom you're referring is Gina?"

Surprised he remembered my mention of her from my few times here, I only nod.

"And I take it by your reaction you believe this is a bad thing?"

I look out the windows, my chest rising and falling quickly, my lips pursed as I fight back my self-loathing. "I don't deserve a woman like her."

Dr. Stein's face furrows with concern. "Why do you think you don't deserve her?"

"Because I'm the one responsible for my fiancée dying."

He sits back in his chair, his thumb and pointer finger forming an L and resting against his cheek and chin. "I thought your fiancée died due to a drunk driver."

In an instant, I'm thrown back to that night three years ago, and I lose all control over my emotions. A tear slides down my cheek as I finally confess, "*She* was the drunk driver."

"What does that have to do with you?"

"I let her leave knowing she was trashed!" I scream, words suddenly bursting forth with an intensity I've never experienced before. "I was angry at her for lying to me. We'd been fighting, and I knew she was fucking drunker than shit and I let her leave anyway. Do you know what could've happened if she'd hit another car instead of a telephone pole that night? I would've been responsible for more deaths!"

Dr. Stein has the decency to let me cry it out, my grief finally releasing the way it probably should've years ago.

When I finally compose myself, he continues. "Walk me through that night. What were you fighting about?"

"We got engaged because she told me she was pregnant. We'd been together almost a year. I'd been thinking about breaking up with her because I started to feel like something was missing in our relationship, even though I thought I loved her. When she told me she was pregnant, I proposed and convinced myself we could make it work. I'd never been in love before so I started thinking maybe it was just me—maybe love just felt that way and there wasn't anything missing. Things still felt off as she started planning the wedding, but I couldn't abandon my kid, so I stuck it out.

"That night,"—I pause, again picturing the ugly scene— "that night, I found out from a buddy she'd been telling her friends, including his girlfriend, that she was going to trap me. We'd only been engaged about a month and she wasn't showing yet. She claimed that was normal, but the reality was she was never pregnant to begin with. Her plan was to tell me after we got married that she had a miscarriage."

"Did you love her?"

I don't even have to think about it. "No. I never loved Candace. At one point, I thought I did, but I know now that wasn't love."

"So, why did you propose then? We live in modern times, where it's fairly common for couples to have a baby out of wedlock."

"I grew up without a father. I had friends whose parents were divorced and only got occasional visitation. I know what that does to a kid. I've never wanted that for my own children, if I ever had them. That's not the kind of father I want to be. I don't want to be a part-time dad. Candace knew that. She knew all about my childhood. She knew about how it impacted me."

"She manipulated you."

I nod.

"And that night you called her on it?"

"Yeah, I came home, and she tried to hide that she'd been drinking. I had been planning to fly to Texas to visit my mom after my game, so she didn't know I was coming home. She was already pretty wasted, but then got belligerent when I called her out for lying about the baby."

"And how did that end with her leaving?"

I sit back against the couch, my eyes closing as I transport myself back to that moment. "I called her a heartless cunt and told her we were done. She lost her mind. She started shrieking at me and slapping my chest calling me a bunch of nasty names. She said I was a great fuck but nothing special, and if I pushed her away, she'd make my life a living hell."

I huff out a hollow laugh. "Seems she did follow through on that one."

"And then she left?"

"No." Guilt laces my words as I continue. "I told her she'd end up alone and no one would love her because she was a selfish bitch with no soul, and I understood why her parents didn't even want her." I drop my face into my hands, my elbows resting on my knees. "I'd never spoken to a woman like that before. My mom would kill me if she knew." I shake my head, shame coursing heavily through me. "She just stood there like I'd slapped her, and then slurred that I'd regret this, grabbed her keys, and walked out. The police showed up two hours later telling me she'd wrapped her car around a telephone pole and died on impact."

I look up, my eyes red and wet. "Her blood alcohol level was .24. They said she was lucky she didn't kill someone else."

"You've been holding onto all this for three years?"

I nod.

"Have you ever told anyone else all of this?"

"No," I whisper.

He leans forward. "Will, what happened to Candace was a tragedy, but it wasn't your fault."

"I should've stopped her from leaving."

His eyes are kind when he looks at me. "In my experience, short of tying her up, which could have potentially put you in a legal mess for holding her against her will, you can't force someone to stay when they are determined to leave, impaired or not."

"I should've taken her keys," I whisper.

"Will, this is not your fault. This was a tragedy, a *horrible* tragedy, but not your fault."

"I don't see how it isn't my fault. I should've found a way to stop her."

He sits back. "Will, what do you need to absolve your guilt?"

"I have no idea. I can't see any way to ever forgive myself for causing her death."

"Then it seems we have our work cut out for us."

THIRTY-TWO

Gina

I walk down Calle del Morro making my way to Castillo San Felipe del Morro, the famous sixteenth-century citadel that has incredible views of the water. It's been years since I've been in Puerto Rico to see my abuela, but I really needed to get out of LA.

Four days ago, I landed in Puerto Rico and got the biggest hug from Abuela, which caused me to immediately burst into tears, something I'm really tired of doing. She's been patient with me, letting me process my heartbreak and not pushing for explanations, but I think it's time I give her some.

But first, I need some fresh air. My daily walks have reacquainted me with Old San Juan, where Abuela lives, but I've been saving my trip to el Castillo for when I felt ready. I used to come here as a little girl and pretend I was a princess in my castle. As an adult, all I keep wishing is that I could finally share the magic of this place with my prince.

My hands rest on a wall overlooking the sea, the open vastness feeling as lonely as I do inside. A tear falls quickly down my cheek, but I don't bother brushing it off. It's not tourist season, so there's really no one around to see my heartache.

I close my eyes, allowing my tears to continue their silent path down my damp cheeks, and take a deep, cleansing breath. The air feels fresher here than LA.

I'm not sure how long I stand there, soaking in the gentle warmth from the sun, my tears slowing until they cease completely. My heart still aches, but I suspect that will last for some time.

Not forever.

But for now.

I reminisce about my childhood vacations to visit my grand-parents and all the times my siblings and I ran around here. Marisol was never into the princess thing, but she indulged my fantasies about how I would be the princess of the castle, with all my servants around me. I smile at the memory. She used to tease me about my dreams of riding off into the sunset with my prince and getting our happily ever after.

Will's face instantly flashes unbidden through my mind.

My heart constricts painfully in my chest.

When will this stop hurting so much?

I spend hours wandering around the castle, forging my childhood memories with new ones. It's different being here as an adult. Everything seems oddly smaller and less extravagant. It's still a beautiful place, a little haunting maybe, but nowhere near as magical as it was when I was a little girl.

Probably because I know fairy tales aren't real.

Not everyone gets their happily ever after.

My walk back to Abuela's is slow. I meander by shops and restaurants, taking in the vast culture represented in this part of Puerto Rico.

As soon as I walk in the door of my abuela's small house, my nose is assaulted with the most delicious smell. God, Abuela can cook. I swear I'm going to go back to LA having gained ten pounds from her cooking.

I walk into the kitchen to see her stirring something in a pot on the stove. When she sees me, her face lights up with a grin, and she wipes her hands on the apron wrapped around her waist as she makes her way to me.

"Ah, Cochita, how was your walk?" She pulls me down to give me a quick kiss on the cheek.

"It was good. I went to el Castillo for a while and then wandered around some local shops." I dip my pinky in the pot to grab a taste before getting a smack on the hand.

"None of that now. I would expect that from your brothers. Dios mío." I smile at her, and she continues, "El Castillo is lovely this time of year. No hay muchas turistas."

"Claro que si. It was very quiet, peaceful almost."

She watches me closely while continuing to stir whatever delicious concoction she's got in the pot.

"So, did you manage to find some peace from your heartache?"

"Abuela," I whisper, my eyes pricking with tears.

"Oh, my sweet Cochita. Dime lo que paso. I hate seeing you so heartbroken."

I look down at the floor, unable to look at her while I open myself up. "I fell in love," I whisper.

"I figured as much. Was he not worthy of you?"

My heart feels like it's being twisted painfully in my chest. God, it hurts to talk about him.

"I thought he was."

"But?"

I sit delicately in the chair at the table by the window. Looking out, I respond, "But I wasn't what he wanted."

"Then he is foolish."

"No, Abuela. He's in love with someone else."

"Who could be better than you, Gina?"

"His fiancée..."

"He's engaged?" she exclaims.

"His fiancée died, and I don't think he's ever gotten over her. His sister suggested as much. She said he was really messed up after Candace died. Candace is the fiancée," I clarify.

"When did she pass away?"

"Three years ago."

"Pobrecito," she whispers, making the sign of the cross and then gripping the delicate gold cross hanging around her neck. It was a gift from my grandfather when they got married. He passed away five years ago, and she hasn't taken it off since. If anyone could understand the inability to stop loving someone, it's her. Maybe she can offer me a unique perspective.

"Do you think you could ever move on from Abuelo?"

Her eyes soften, and she cups my cheek, gently wiping away an escaped tear I didn't even notice. "Your abuelo and I were together for over fifty years. It's very different than never being married to someone. I have no doubt he loved her. You don't propose to someone you don't love, but I think he could someday be ready to love again."

"Just not with me," my voice cracks as another tear escapes. I brush it aside quickly, wishing that crying didn't make me feel so weak.

Abuela's eyes tear up. "It hurts me to see you in such pain."

"I'll be okay."

"Don't lie to me. You forget, you and I are a lot alike. We love with our whole heart."

I look into her eyes. "I thought I loved Collin, but my feelings for Will are so much stronger. I didn't even feel this devastated when I discovered Collin cheating on me."

"I never liked Collin. I wish I could've met your Will."

Your Will.

Oh, Abuela, I wish he was mine.

But his heart belongs to someone else, and nothing I do will ever change that.

"Thank you for letting me stay here with you for a while. There were too many memories in LA."

"You know I always love when you visit, but running away from your problems won't solve them. You'll eventually need to go back to LA, and what will you do then?"

I look out the window, pondering her question. When she realizes I'm not going to answer—or can't—she rubs my shoulder and then goes back to the stove. I look out at the streets of Old San Juan thinking about her question. What will I do when I go back to LA?

I'll work, visit with friends, and attempt to avoid any possible run-ins with Will. Of course, there's the added challenge that my best friend is engaged to one of his teammates, and we're both invited to their wedding. I have no idea how I'll handle being in the same room with Will while I'm supposed to be happy for my friend and pretend I'm not completely heartbroken.

God, that's going to be torture. I'm going to need a date to act as a buffer, or I'll never survive.

I can manage to live in the same city without being drawn to Will, but there's no way I'll manage being in the same room as him and not want his thick arms wrapped around me.

"So, how long are you planning to hide away?"

I turn to my abuela. "I was thinking two more weeks. Most of my work can be done remotely, and Victoria, my boss, offered me a travel series, so I can feature Puerto Rico first if I decide to take it."

"Does a travel series mean you'd go to those places?"

"Yeah,"—I shrug—"it's not really what I want to write, though."

"But you're considering it because it'll allow you to keep running away from your pain."

Damn. She really does know me.

I purse my lips and nod reluctantly. "Something like that."

"Gina, be careful. If you keep running, how will you know when to stop?"

Her words pierce through the armor I've been trying to build, causing it to crumble around me. She's right.

If I keep running, I'll never stop.

And then I'll be no better than Will—in love with someone I can't have.

I deserve more than that. I want a better life than one with no roots.

With that thought, my pain starts to slowly subside, allowing me to embrace the possibility that maybe, just maybe, my prince is still out there.

Waiting for me.

THIRTY-THREE

Will

Dr. Stein watches me closely. "How did it go?"

"I couldn't do it."

He squints subtly. "Why do you think that is?"

I shrug.

"Will, you've been seeing me three times a week for the past two weeks. You've opened up about things you never revealed in our previous sessions. We've gone over how important this is for you to take the next step in working through your guilt."

"I know."

"So, what's holding you back?"

I take a deep breath and look out the window while I ponder his question. I wish I had a good answer, but I don't.

"I don't know."

"I think you do."

Frustration, and an all too familiar anger, seeps through my bones. "It's not that simple! I don't know why I can't go there."

"Take a breath, Will, and tell me what you're feeling right now."

I do as he asks, sorting through the frustration and anger to find the emotion that is the root of it all. "Fear," I whisper.

He gets a contemplative look on his face. "Fear about what?"

I hesitate, trying to pinpoint what exactly is driving this feeling. "That it won't make a goddamn difference. That I'll be right back where I started." I take a breath. "That none of it will matter in the long run."

"You mean if it doesn't help you get Gina back?"

My shoulders sag. "I think that ship has already sailed, Doc."

"Then why do you continue to include her in your reasoning for pushing through this? It's not lost on me that you came back to therapy because she left you. Based on what you've said these past couple of weeks, you still love her."

"Of course I still love her. She's the best woman I've ever known. Fuck, she's the *only* woman I've ever been in love with." I have no doubts anymore that what I feel for Gina is real love, not the lust and infatuation I once confused for love with Candace.

"So, what are you going to do about it?"

I know what he's implying. He firmly believes I need to complete this next step in order to heal and open myself up to Gina and give her what I know she really needs.

We watch each other, neither saying a word, but a silent conversation passes between us nonetheless.

He's right. If I want even a sliver of a chance at getting Gina back, then I need to do this.

"Alright. I'll go."

He nods and folds his hands in his lap. "Can't wait to hear about it at our session on Friday."

The grass is a deep green from the endless amount of water they use to keep the place looking immaculate. *Don't they know California is in a perpetual drought?* It seems silly to waste so much water on those who don't appreciate it.

But I guess it's more for those who come to visit, not those lying in the ground.

The cemetery is quiet, only birds flying in the sky making much noise. I had to go in the office to ask where I could find her grave since I never came to the funeral. I make my way over to a large Chinese elm tree shadowing the grass. She's in an isolated part of the cemetery about twenty feet from the narrow road that loops around. I look down at the different names, searching for hers.

My breath catches in my chest when I see her name on the slate-gray grave marker.

Candace Beckwin.

God, it's been so long since I've seen her name. I've thought it, but seeing it is like a punch to the gut. Despite her parents' wealth, they were cheap and just bought a simple marker that lies flat in the ground. Even in death, they neglect her.

I squat down, gently placing the small bundle of ivory roses on her grave. They were her favorite.

Emotion bubbles in my throat, attempting to break out. Doc warned me this would happen, but experiencing it is something else entirely. He told me not to fight it.

Easier said than done.

I close my eyes and inhale the crisp late fall air. Unbidden by me, a warm drop of water slides down my cheeks as I release the breath and my emotions along with it.

That one tear is all it takes to open the floodgates.

I cover my eyes with my hand and let go, finally releasing all the pain and guilt I've held close to my heart for the past three years.

Swiping my hand down my face in a weak attempt to slow the tears, I choke out, "I'm so fucking sorry, Candace."

More tears fall, my pain hitting me with a force it hasn't done since I found out she died. I fall back on my ass, sitting in the dewy grass, my arms draped over my now bent knees and my chin tucked against my chest.

Time moves on, like it always does, while I sit there at a complete standstill. Memories slam into me, from the first time I met Candace to the last time I saw her, her words slurred and tears streaming down her cheeks, her makeup a hideous mess on her normally immaculately done up face.

Sitting here, my memories seem different than they used to. Instead of seeing hate and anger in her eyes during our fight, I see her pain—the same pain she had when we first met. She attempted to hide it and did a damn good job of it, but looking back, it was there the entire time.

I wonder why I never noticed before. Was she really that unhappy the whole time we were together? I think back on the conversations where she would open up a little about her family —she was almost always drunk. She would confess how much their neglect made her feel worthless. Was that why she always drank so much?

Was that why she lied about the baby and tried to trap me in a marriage where we both would've ended up miserable?

"I wish you could give me answers," I whisper, my voice still scratchy from all the crying. "I need to let you go, Candace. I don't want to be miserable anymore."

An image of Gina's smiling face breaks through my melancholy.

My voice strengthens. "I want to be happy. I want to love her the way she deserves."

I hear a birdsong in the tree above me and look up. A little, brown bird sits there, looking right at me. It chirps and then flies down to sit right on Candace's grave.

Is this some kind of message? Or have I officially lost my mind?

The bird sings its short song, looking at me the entire time, and then flies away. I watch it soar into the cloudy gray sky.

I look back at Candace's grave feeling oddly lighter, like that little bird took all my guilt, pain, and hate with it. Well, maybe not all of it—that'll come with time and more sessions with Dr. Stein—but enough that it doesn't feel like such a burden anymore.

Ignoring the dampness of my pants from the wet grass, I sit forward and gently place my hand on her grave.

"I really am sorry for everything. But I need to let you go now."

I stand up, brush off my pants, and with one last look, turn and walk out of the cemetery, my long-held guilt now buried in the ground with Candace and no longer holding tight to my heart.

"So, were you able to go to the cemetery?"

"Yeah."

"And how was it?"

"Freeing."

Dr. Stein smiles. "Care to elaborate, or are you going to leave me hanging?"

I smirk. "Actually, I think it's time we move on to what's important."

He looks at me curiously. "And what would that be? I thought moving on from your guilt was important to you?"

"It was, but I don't feel guilty anymore. You were right, I

should've gone to see Candace a long time ago. When I left the cemetery, I left my guilt behind with her. I feel freer than I have since I first met Candace."

"I'm very happy to hear that, Will." His soft smile changes into a curious look. "So then, what's important now?"

"How do I get Gina back?"

THIRTY-FOUR

Gina

I hug my abuela tight, knowing it'll probably be months, if not longer, before I see her again. She squeezes me back and leaves a kiss on my cheek.

"Thank you for letting me visit for so long."

She cups my cheek with her small, delicate hand. "Cochita, you are welcome to come visit me any time. Just try to come visit when you're not running away from something, sí?"

"I will. Te quiero."

"Te quiero tambien."

"Benedicíon."

She holds my hands, giving a gentle squeeze as she gives me the traditional blessing, "Que dios te bendiga."

I wrap my arms around her, holding her close and praying she can feel how thankful I am for this time with her. I fight back a tear as I walk through the terminal to my flight.

The journey to LA is long, nearly eleven hours with a brief layover in Miami. When the plane finally touches down at LAX, the rock in the pit of my stomach returns at the thought that I'm now back in the same city as Will.

No. I'm done thinking about him.

I promised myself before I left Puerto Rico that I was going to move on. The right man for me is still out there, I just haven't found him yet. I need to keep believing that someday, when the time is right, we'll find each other, and for once I'll find a man who doesn't break my heart. I nod my head at my thoughts, hoping if I just say it enough, then I'll finally stop wishing Will were that man.

I exit the airport and find a familiar face waiting for me.

"Hey, stranger," Paige says, a small smile on her face.

"Hey, thanks for picking me up."

"Of course! What are friends for if not to put up with the God-awful mess that is LAX?"

I laugh and then quickly wrap my best friend in a tight hug. I've missed her. We've talked over the phone and even Face-Time, but it's not the same as seeing her in person. She helps me get my luggage in the trunk of her car and then we attempt to maneuver our way through the clusterfuck that is this airport. It takes us thirty minutes, but we finally get to the freeway and take the 405 to my apartment.

"So, how was it seeing your grandma?"

I smile, thinking about the past three weeks. "It was really great. There's so much history there, and I forgot how good of a cook Abuela is."

"Um..." she begins but hesitates, and I turn to her. Her gaze is cautious when she glances at me, and I notice she's chewing on the inside of her lip.

"What?"

"Did you think about Will while you were there?"

Oh.

Damn, I was hoping she wouldn't ask about him right away.

I turn toward the front window to watch the traffic in front of us. "I did, and I came to the realization he wasn't the man for me. Didn't Oprah once say when someone tells you who they are, you should believe them? Well, clearly, I should've taken her advice. From the beginning, Will made it clear he didn't want me."

Her face scrunches up. "First of all, I'm pretty sure that quote was Maya Angelou, not Oprah. Second, I completely disagree with you."

"Disagree all you want, but you can't deny he kept fighting against it, against the weird chemistry we had together. He didn't *want* to like me."

"If he didn't want you, then why the hell would he date you? You two were perfect for each other."

I know Paige is trying to help, but her words cut me deeply. I've just spent the last three weeks convincing myself we *weren't* perfect for each other. I need her to be on the same page with me, especially after she promised she wouldn't push him on me anymore.

"Paige, please don't."

She quickly glances at me, worry in her eyes. "Don't what?"

"Don't pretend Will and I were anything but a brief sexual encounter. In the grand scheme of my life, Will won't mean anything."

"Are you sure about that? I mean, is that really what you want?"

"It doesn't matter what I want."

Her gaze leaves the road and meets with mine briefly. "Of course it does. What do you want, Gina?"

I look back out the window, thinking about it.

"You really want to know?"

I catch her nod from the corner of my eye.

"I want a man who puts me first. I want a man who loves me unconditionally. I want to finally be enough, just as I am."

"What if you *are* all those things for Will?"

I close my eyes, pain slicing through me. "Paige, stop. Please," I whisper.

I turn to her, my eyes pleading with her. "It hurts too much to talk about this. Please let it go. Will and I are over. You promised you wouldn't do this anymore."

She glances back over at me but finally stops talking. I turn on the radio and we spend the rest of the trip listening to the Top 40 pop songs, both of us lost in our own thoughts.

The closer we get to my apartment, the more I notice Paige glancing over at me nervously, her fingers fidgeting along the steering wheel. Finally, I can't take it anymore.

"What is wrong with you? You're acting like you're about to be busted for drugs or something."

She chews her lips and squeezes the steering wheel just as we pull up to my apartment.

"Don't hate me," she says.

My brow furrows in confusion. "Why would I hate you?"

Her gaze moves from me to something behind me. I turn my head and my heart plummets to my stomach. Sitting on the stairs leading to my apartment is none other than the man I just spent the last three weeks trying to get over.

"What the hell?" I whisper.

He stands up, his gaze clashing with mine, and my heart starts beating furiously in my chest.

I turn to Paige and catch her guilty expression. "Did you have something to do with this?"

She chews on her lip again. "Kinda."

"Kinda?" I point out the window toward the stairs. "How is *that* kinda?"

"Gina, please don't be mad. When Will came over a couple of days ago, I was ready to kick him right out again for what he did to you, but Jack made me listen to what he had to say. You need to hear him out."

"What happened to girl code? You're supposed to be on my side!"

"I am on your side. You'll understand once you talk to him. Trust me."

"Trust you?"

She glares at me. "Have I ever steered you wrong? Do you seriously think I would do this if I thought he was just going to hurt you more?"

No, she wouldn't. I shake my head, my words stuck in my throat.

She gets out and goes around to the trunk to grab my luggage. I take a deep breath and then open my door to meet her at the back of her car. She pulls my large suitcase out, then closes the lid.

"I promise you—I really think this will make things better."

I look at her doubtfully, but don't say anything. She asked me to trust her, so that's what I'm trying to do. Instead, I lean in and pull her into a hug, thanking her for picking me up and bringing me home. She gives me one more squeeze, then gets back in her car and drives away.

I watch her car until she turns a corner and disappears. Then with one more deep breath and a quick prayer for strength, I turn to Will.

My steps are slow, my feet feeling heavy like lead. My eyes stay down since the idea of looking at him is painful. Even just the few glimpses I've gotten so far have felt like a stab to the heart.

Within moments I'm standing in front of him. When he doesn't say anything, I finally look up. The second our gazes connect, pain grips my heart and tears sting the back of my eyes.

I will not cry in front of him. I will not cry.

I don't speak. I can't. If I open my mouth right now, I'll either burst into tears or want to punch him.

"Gina, I..." his voice cracks, and I get a small pleasure knowing this is just as hard on him as it is on me.

He clears his throat and tries again. "I had a whole speech planned, but the moment I saw you, all the words disappeared." His eyes roam over my face. "God, I've fucking missed you." He lifts his hands like he wants to grab me and pull me to him, but I step back, out of his reach.

I shake my head twice, and then continue to stand there staring at him. I want to ask him why he's here, but I still can't speak.

He swallows and rubs the scruff on his face with his hand. "Gina, I want to explain everything."

I fortify my resolve to get through this and finally find my voice. "There's no need, Will. I understand."

I'm proud of how my voice holds strong. I take a step to the side, attempting to walk around him toward my apartment, but he sidesteps in front of me, his hand reaching out to keep me from walking past him.

"You don't."

I look at him, confused. "What?"

"You don't understand. You think you do, but you don't. I owe you an explanation, and I'm ready to talk about everything. I've been working through a lot of things with my therapist."

That information surprises me.

"You've been seeing a therapist?" Most men I know look down on therapy, like they're too good for it and it's only for crazy people. Little do they know, sometimes it really helps to get perspective from a neutral party. I had no idea Will even went to therapy.

My heart sinks at the realization that it just confirms how little I know him. We were dating for two months, and I didn't even know he was seeing a therapist.

How can I love someone I don't even know?

He nods in response to my question. "Yeah, I saw him for a while when we first started dating and then started up again when we broke up."

"Well, I'm glad you've been able to work through things. Now, if you'll excuse me."

He reaches out. "Please, just give me five minutes. If you don't want to hear any more after five minutes, then I'll leave and you'll never have to see me again."

His eyes pierce mine, desperation in their depths.

I look down at the ground hoping to figure out if I can manage five more minutes in his presence. Already, I can feel my walls crumbling, my love for him rising to the forefront and practically begging me to hear him out.

Five minutes. *I can survive five minutes more and then I'll never have to see him again.*

The thought doesn't offer me any comfort, but my mind is made up.

"Fine. Five minutes, but let's go inside. It's cold out here."

He nods. "Okay."

Without asking, he grabs my suitcase and starts up the stairs. I stand there, my jaw slack and my indignation rising.

I can carry my own damn suitcase.

I huff out a breath and remind myself it's only five minutes before following him up the stairs.

Once we get into my apartment, I set my keys in the dish on the table by the door and hang up my coat. When I turn around, Will is walking out of my room empty-handed.

"I put your suitcase by your bed."

"Thanks." I wrap my arms around my torso. "So, you wanted to explain?"

He gestures to the couch. "Can we sit?"

On the same couch? Doubtful. But it's not like I have a lot of seating options in my small apartment, so it'll have to do. I sit down at the far end of the couch, burrowing in the corner with my back hugging the arm in an attempt to remain as far away from him as possible.

He either doesn't notice or ignores it altogether, because he sits more on the middle cushion than the far cushion, and his sandalwood scent washes over me.

Damn him for smelling so good.

"Your time is running out."

"What?"

"You've been in here for at least three minutes."

"The deal was you'd give me five minutes to talk."

"Yeah, but you aren't using it to talk."

"My five minutes don't start until I start talking."

I roll my eyes. "Fine, then start talking so we can get this over with."

I don't miss the pain that flashes in his eyes at my callous comment, but I hide my remorse by hugging my arms around my body tighter.

He rubs his hands together in front of him and turns his head toward me. "I was never in love with Candace."

I can't hide the shock that covers my face. "What?"

"I didn't love her. Not really. For a long time, I thought I did, but the last few months we were together things were strained, and I always felt like something was missing."

"But you proposed to her..."

"She said she was pregnant. You know how I grew up. I never wanted that for my own kid. I had no intention of being a part-time dad."

"No, you wouldn't do that after what your dad did to you guys."

He offers me a soft smile, his eyes showing clear appreciation that I understand him.

"So, you were going to have a baby?"

"No."

"Okay, I'm confused. You just said—"

"She lied. She was never pregnant."

"Oh my God, Will."

"I know. She could tell I was pulling away and wanted to trap me, or at least that's what she told the girlfriend of a buddy of mine. I was furious when I found out."

"I can imagine you would be." I run my hand through my hair and then cover my mouth, picturing it clearly—Will dedicating himself to a potentially loveless marriage to be a good father and then finding out she was manipulating him. Any man would be angry.

"When I got home that night, she wasn't expecting me. She was drunk, totally smashed, which tipped me off that my buddy's girlfriend had been telling the truth. We got in a huge fight. I said a lot of things I regret. Nasty, horrible things. My mother would be ashamed if she knew I ever spoke to a woman that way. But I was so angry, and she was so cold and heartless about it all. When she grabbed her keys and left, I didn't stop her, even though I knew she was too drunk to drive. I mean, fuck, she was slurring her words and could barely string a sentence together by the time she walked out the door."

Oh, God. I think I know where this is going.

"A couple of hours after she left, a police officer showed up and told me she had wrapped her car around a telephone pole and died instantly."

"Oh, Will." I reach out and place my hand on his arm, because I can't stop myself from offering him comfort right now, regardless of how much he's hurt me.

He places his hand over mine and squeezes, his eyes red-rimmed when they meet mine. "I blamed myself. For three years, I blamed myself for her death. If I'd stopped her, she wouldn't have died. I thought I deserved to be alone and miserable."

"Will, it was a terrible accident. You weren't in the right frame of mind that night either. You can't blame yourself."

He nods. "I'm learning to accept that now. For the longest time, I just tried to bury everything I was feeling, although the guilt was always there gnawing away at me. I never told anyone what happened, except that she died. I never confessed she hadn't been pregnant or that we fought that night. I almost slipped with Jack once, enough that he always thought there was more to the story, but he never pushed. My sister doesn't even know."

Woah. He and Becka are incredibly close. I would've expected he'd tell her first.

"Does she know now?"

He shakes his head. "Not yet. My therapist knows, as well as Jack and Paige because it was the only way I could get Paige on board to help me, and now you."

"Why me?"

His thumb glides over the top of my hand still resting on his arm. "A year after Candace died, I got roped into going to dinner with Jack and this girl he was interested in."

I smile, already knowing this story.

"Lo and behold, her absolutely stunning best friend was with her." His eyes lock on mine, vulnerability shining through. "Gina, from the first moment I saw you, you threw me off balance. You forced me to feel things I didn't think I deserved to feel after what I did. That's why I kept trying to push you away. That night at the candy store? I was so tired of fighting it. I just wanted to be with you, to feel you in my arms. And then the mom yelled at her little girl. She called out the name Candace, and it was like a bucket of ice water got tossed on me."

I think back to that night, looking at it with new eyes. I

remember the mother and daughter, but I hadn't been paying any attention to her name, my focus solely on Will.

"Then, I got moved to second string at the start of the season and decided it was time to see a therapist. I couldn't lose football because then I'd really have nothing. I'd worked through some things with him early on, enough that when you moved down here, I knew I didn't want to stay away from you. I wanted to give this an honest shot. I wanted to be with you in every way possible."

I offer him a small smile. "Which you did."

He smiles back. "Yeah. And it was perfect."

"I wondered if you were still in love with Candace," I say softly, looking down at our joined hands. "You dreamed of her."

He squeezes my hand. When I still don't look at him, he gently lifts my face. "I wasn't in love with her, and those weren't dreams. They were nightmares. I truly had never been happier than I was with you."

"Then why did you pull away again?"

Now it's Will's turn to look down. "Because Jack said I looked like a man in love."

My heart stops.

"I realized he was right." He looks me in the eyes, his own full of love and longing.

"What?" I barely manage to whisper the word.

"I love you, Gina."

I shake my head. "But you pushed me away."

He shakes his head and cups my cheek. "Because it scared the shit out of me. What I feel for you is so much more than I've ever felt for anyone, and I freaked out. But I don't want to be the guy that runs away from you. I can't. I love you so fucking much that these past three weeks have been the worst of my life. Nothing means anything without you. I don't want to hide from you anymore. I want to be the man you deserve. No one will ever love you as much as I do. I'm sorry it took me so long to get my shit figured out. I hate that I hurt you, but I will do anything in my power to make it up to you if you'll give me another chance."

Tears slide down my cheeks at his confession.

"You love me?"

"I do." He brushes a tear from my cheek. "Do you think you could ever love me?"

I look into his eyes, my heart beating profusely in my chest. Am I really about to put myself on the line like this?

"I'm afraid to."

His eyes soften. "Why?"

"Because I don't want you to do your little switch thing and turn into Cold Will again."

The resolve in his voice is undeniable. "I promise you, Cold Will is gone for good. I won't be that guy with you ever again, Gina. That's not the life I want with you."

I want to believe him. I'm desperate to believe him. "How can you be sure you won't push me away again?"

He cups my cheek, his gaze penetrating mine, allowing his vulnerability to shine through. "I pushed you away because of my own guilt and insecurities. But I don't feel guilty anymore, and I'm still working with my therapist to make sure I work through my problems instead of letting them interfere with my life. So, I can guarantee I won't push you away again, because that is the last thing I want. I want you, Gina, any way you'll let me have you. And I'll do whatever it takes to prove my love to you."

He takes a breath and then whispers, "Can you ever forgive me? For hurting you, and for pushing you away?"

I squeeze his hand, all the pain we've both endured these past few weeks easing away into the background. "I already have. It helped, hearing you explain everything." I realize the truth of my words after I say them. His explanation and his clear devotion make it easy to forgive him. Doesn't mean it isn't scary giving him another chance—it is, especially since we don't have the greatest track record—but isn't love a risk in itself? Despite all my fears, concerns, and protests, my heart belongs to him. Completely.

"What will it take?"

"For what?"

"For your heart."

God, this man. Doesn't he realize he already owns it?

"It's already yours," I whisper.

Hope fills his gaze. "Does that mean you *are* willing to try this? To be a couple again?"

"You're sure that's what you want?"

"I want whatever you'll give me, but in a perfect world, yes, I want you, all of you. I want you to be mine."

"Okay," I say quietly.

His eyes light up. "Okay?"

I nod. "On one condition."

"Name it."

THIRTY-FIVE

Will

"OH FUCK, WILL!!!"

Gina screaming my name through her climax has to be one of the hottest things I've ever encountered.

I lift my head from between her thighs, my lips wet from her release as she comes back down.

"You sure you can handle more?"

She breathes heavily. "Yes...just...give me a few minutes. Fuck, your tongue should be illegal." She tilts her head up to look down at me. "But don't think I'm not still aware you owe me five more orgasms."

"As you wish."

An exhausted smile graces her beautiful face before she drops her head back to the bed. She thinks owing her so many orgasms without my own release is punishment—okay, maybe it is a little because, fuck, watching her come makes me harder than stone—but I could do this all day and never tire of seeing her orgasm crashing through her.

If this is how she plans to punish me for the rest of our lives, then I'm one lucky man.

The crowd screams loudly in the background as Jack shouts out the play. He looks at me sharply. "Think you can do this?"

Oh, fuck yeah.

I nod. "You can count on me."

He nods back and we bump fists before he breaks up the huddle. Our offensive line gets in position, waiting for the play to begin.

In seconds, the ball is hiked back to Jack, and I take off like a shot. My legs burn and my abs clench as I push my body farther down the field. I see an opening right where I need it and take a sharp right hook toward the middle of the field, just barely dodging a tackle by a linebacker. Pushing my body further, I turn my head back and see the ball spiraling through the air.

I'm almost there.

With one last push, I jump up and catch the ball as it soars across the middle of the field. Adrenaline spikes through my body as I grip it securely in my hands and bring it close to my chest, holding it with everything I've got, knowing if I drop the ball now, I'll be letting my team down.

My feet land on the ground, the ball held snugly against my chest as I see two defenders barreling toward me. I brace myself for impact knowing it doesn't matter now.

I got the ball.

I've already proven my worthiness.

At the end of the game, Coach Denton passes me the game-winning ball.

"You earned this. You've really turned it around this year, Edmonson. I think you're playing better than when we drafted you. Keep it up, son."

He pats me on the back and walks to his office.

I twirl the game ball in my hands and then glance up to see Jack looking at me from his cubby with a grin on his face.

"Feels good, doesn't it?"

I shrug. "I've won a game ball before."

He shakes his head, his grin turning into a full smile at my ignorance.

"What?" I ask.

"She makes everything feel a hundred times better, doesn't she?"

I look down at the ball, remembering the high I got when we won the game and my role in our victory. I think back over the past few weeks that Gina and I have been back together and how everything seems brighter, tastes better, feels stronger.

I look up at my friend, a smile spreading across my face. "Yeah, she does."

Matt turns from his cubby, clearly having eavesdropped on our conversation. "So, when are you going to pop the question?"

I shake my head, my smile still bright on my face. "Depends."

His brow furrows. "On what?"

"On whether or not we go to the Super Bowl."

Matt and Jack both smile and then go back to getting changed. I turn to my cubby and glance inside at the small velvet box holding the ring I bought after Gina and I got back together.

I know, without a doubt in my mind, we are meant to be together.

She's mine.

And I'm hers.

Forever.

The End

Want to see Will's proposal?
Sign up for my newsletter for the bonus epilogue!

Thank you for reading Across the Middle! Matt and Nikki's
story is coming soon.
Order Down by Contact today!
Keep reading for a preview of Chapter 1.

Join my Facebook reader group, Cadence Keys Book Lovers, for
exclusive giveaways and sneak peeks of future books.

DOWN BY CONTACT PREVIEW

Chapter 1: Nikki

I look at the marketing materials sitting before me and shake my head. *This has to be some kind of mistake.*

"Luther, you can't be serious," I stare at him in disbelief. "You want Matt Fischer to lead the new Wolves campaign?"

Luther, the best in the marketing and promotions department, and one of my dearest friends, nods his head. "Definitely. The group testing confirmed he's the way to go for our campaign this year. He's on fire this season and he's hotter than ever. Women want to be with him and men want to *be* him. This is definitely his time to shine."

I shudder and look back down at the face of the one man on the team I can't stand. His pretty boy features on that insanely strong, defined, athletic body really shouldn't be allowed. And don't even get me started on his piercing blue eyes and the charming smile he tosses at every woman.

"He's practically a walking STD. The last thing the Wolves need is to tie our brand to one of our most notoriously slutty players. He's an unabashed womanizer." I force my gaze from the picture of Matt's ridiculously handsome face, ignoring the slight uptick in my heartbeat, and stare sternly at Luther. "No, we should definitely go with someone more wholesome. What about Jack Fuller?"

He shakes his head, "Jack has done several campaigns for us, but he's pulling back in preparation for his wedding to Paige. Plus, the group tests showed that while everyone loves him, because he's the NFL's golden boy, they much preferred Matt. I'm telling you, he was the choice by a landslide."

I wrack my brain for another alternative, *anyone* who might be a better draw than Matt "Manwhore" Fischer. But no names come to mind. It's a lot harder than one would think to find a wholesome player on our team. They're good guys, but they definitely get around.

My shoulders sag in defeat. You'd think on a team of 53 players we'd be able to find one that isn't the biggest ladies' man on the team.

I groan and fight the urge to bang my head on my clean and meticulously organized cherry wood desk. "Is he seriously our only decent option?"

Luther just smiles at me like he thinks I'm adorably naïve. "Sex sells, Nikki. Let's give the people what they want."

I throw my head back and take a centering breath, already dreading the next few months where I'll have to work closely with Matt. As the lead of the marketing and promotions department, I don't normally have to interact with the players – that's a task I can designate to someone else – but as Coach Denton's only daughter, I've met and interacted with pretty much every player on the team.

Out of all the players my dad has ever coached, no one has ever rubbed me the wrong way like Matt Fischer does. From the very first time I met him and he threw me that stupidly charming smirk, I knew he was trouble with a capital T. I'll never forget his warm voice floating over me and the way my blood heated and tingled in ways it never has, or the way my breath stuttered momentarily in my chest before his words finally registered. "Well, well, well, who do we have here? Hands off boys, I call dibs. Come on over here, honey, and sit on my face."

Needless to say, I think he's a disgusting chauvinistic pig and he thinks I'm a stuck-up princess. I'm already wishing I could speed up time and get these next three months over with.

I walk into my house and line up my shoes in the shoe caddy by the front door. Rubbing the tight muscles in my neck, I attempt to work out the tension that's been growing since my conversation with Luther. I walk through the hallways of my house, barely noticing the ostentatious artwork Anthony insisted we get when we were decorating our new house. It looks like a kindergartner threw paint on a canvas. I still can't believe the outrageous price Anthony paid for it, but he claims the artist is someone up and coming. Anthony loves to be ahead of the trends. Personally, I'd rather have gotten some artwork with more landscapes, or something calming.

But Anthony was insistent, and it didn't seem like it was worth arguing over. If there's anything I've learned in my life, it's that you have to pick your battles.

I walk into the kitchen, stalling slightly when I see Anthony standing near the stove, stirring a pot of something that smells delicious. Anthony never cooks for me.

"What's the special occasion?" I ask, walking toward him, a surprised smile on my face as I take in the aroma of whatever he's cooking.

He turns to me, "What do you mean?"

"You're cooking."

He shrugs, "So? I cook."

My smile falters as he turns back to the pot. "Not usually for me. You usually order us takeout."

"Only when I know you're too tired to clean the kitchen. But I figured you'd be willing to clean up tonight since you have tomorrow off."

I stare at him, my smile now completely gone, half expecting him to tell me he's joking.

"It's not like I have the day off to lounge around the house, Anthony." I can't hide the tension in my voice. My breaths are already coming in short pants as I try to fight the emotion bubbling up in my chest.

He doesn't even turn to look at me this time. "True, but you won't be at the cemetery all day. Just for part of it. I'm sure even your folks don't want to spend their whole day there."

I can't respond to his comment, for fear I'll scream at him for his insensitivity to what tomorrow means to me. And screaming isn't something I do. I'm nothing if not composed and competent, always.

It's why Anthony loves me. At least that's one of the few reasons he's given me for why he wants to marry me.

The wine fridge under the counter to my right catches my eye, so instead of trying to come up with some semblance of a response, I grab a wine glass from the cabinet and open up a bottle of red wine – not paying any attention to the brand of the bottle in my hand. I pour a generous amount into my glass and then take a large, fortifying sip.

"You really should let that air out to get the full robust flavors. That's too good a year to waste."

I can feel the cracks in my carefully composed foundation beginning to crumble. Ignoring Anthony's advice, I mumble a lame excuse about not being hungry and take my wine upstairs to our giant master bedroom. Frankly, I think this house is too big for just the two of us, but Anthony wanted something appropriate for our wealth, and, like I always do, I went with it.

I place my wine glass on my nightstand and slip out of my blouse and skirt, throwing them in the hamper because I know how much Anthony hates it when I leave my clothes on the floor. I slide off my panty hose, grab my wine glass, taking a generous gulp when I do, and walk into our luxurious bathroom wearing my matching cream bra and underwear.

Standing in front of the mirror, I stare at the woman looking back at me. I set my wine glass on the counter and brace my hands against the white and gray marble sink hoping to relieve the weight of this burden I carry, if only for a moment. A tear slides down my pale cheek, and my gaze stares back at me, red rimmed, and swirling with all the pain I normally keep buried so no one will know how I really feel.

A heavy breath leaves my chest as I exhale slowly, working to compose myself in case Anthony comes up here. I take one more for good measure before washing my face and making myself a bubble bath so I can ease some of the stress from today. But I know it's pointless because tomorrow will come with its own unique stress.

Tomorrow is the anniversary of my sister's death. The one day a year when my family and I go to her grave. I go on my own sometimes – although not often – as I'm sure my parents do, but the anniversary is always a day when we go and relive the pain of losing her together.

As I immerse myself in the hot, lavender and peppermint scented bubbly water and take another generous sip of my wine, I ponder what my life could've been like if things had been different. If my sister hadn't died that day so many years ago. If my role in her death didn't eat me alive.

I quickly shut down that thought.

Things aren't different.

This is the bed I've made myself, and now I need to sleep in it.

Whether I like it or not.

Pre-order Now
Releasing June 3, 2021

ACKNOWLEDGMENTS

There are always so many people who work behind the scenes to make a book possible and I've been incredibly fortunate to make some wonderful friendships on this author journey of mine.

Romance Newbies: I could thank you endlessly and it still wouldn't feel like enough. You are all so amazing and talented and I feel honored to be among you. Love you all <3!

Romance Support Group: There are some days our chat thread makes me laugh so hard that any problems I'm stressing about fly right out the window. Keep those dirty pictures coming ladies ;)

Marisol, thank you so much for sharing your Puerto Rican culture with me and guiding me as I wrote this story. It was so important to me that Gina be authentic and her culture is such a big part of who she is. I couldn't have incorporated that critical piece of her without all your help.

Kate, you make the best damn covers. THANK YOU!

My editors, Ann and Ann, I can't begin to offer you enough thanks for all your help with this book. But I will say, I'm sorry for all the nods. :)

Rikki, thank you for always being my person and being the first person I ever trusted to read my stories.

To my hubby, literally none of this would be possible without you. Thank you for believing in me even when I don't believe in myself. Thank you for loving me when I'm difficult and for pushing me to chase this crazy dream. I'm so grateful for everything you do for our family.

Baby K, thank you for being the miracle that you are. I love you more than words. You are the greatest gift I've ever been given.

And to you, for actually reading this book (and making it through the acknowledgements). I really couldn't do any of this without you buying my books and loving my stories. Thank you so much for your support.

ABOUT THE AUTHOR

Cadence Keys writes steamy contemporary romance novels full of heart, heat, and HEAs. She loves football (especially seeing all those tight ends), coffee (it sustains her), and watching Gilmore Girl marathons (witty banter for the win). She has been writing for almost a decade, but only recently got the gumption to really do something with her work. She looks forward to publishing many more novels.

You can also find more information about all future releases at www.cadencekeysauthor.com/

facebook.com/cadencekeysauthor
twitter.com/cadencewrites
instagram.com/cadencekeysauthor
bookbub.com/profile/cadence-keys
goodreads.com/cadencekeysauthor
amazon.com/Cadence-Keys/e/B08H8SXT9D/ref=dp_byline_cont_pop_ebooks_1